For the reading of Bobby's will, the attorneys sat Vanessa, the ex, Bobby and Vanessa's daughter Roberta, and me in a conference room together. I was instructed to bring a lawyer as were the other two ladies. I didn't. That sort of thing isn't in me. Vanessa did. The lawyer read Bobby's will. It was pretty much as I expected. I got the house we shared and most of the money accounts; Roberta received two hundred thousand dollars in a fund her father had set aside for her upon his death. Then, the lawyer read further. Bobby did something none of us expected. He gave me half the interest in the diner and the other half to Vanessa! Just like Bobby to be equitable.

Bobby's Diner

by

Susan Wingate

The Bobby's Diner Series

Bobby's Diner

Cover Art by *Diane Carlile*

The Wild Rose Press, Inc.
PO Box 708
Adams Basin, NY 14410-0708
Visit us at www.thewildrosepress.com

Publishing History
First Edition, 2021
Trade Paperback ISBN 978-1-5092-3515-5
Digital ISBN 978-1-5092-3516-2

The Bobby's Diner Series
Published in the United States of America

Dedication

For Bob

Chapter 1

For the reading of Bobby's will, the attorneys sat Vanessa, the ex, Bobby and Vanessa's daughter Roberta, and me in a conference room together. I was instructed to bring a lawyer as were the other two ladies. I didn't. That sort of thing isn't in me. Vanessa did. The lawyer read Bobby's will. It was pretty much as I expected. I got the house we shared and most of the money accounts; Roberta received two hundred thousand dollars in a fund her father had set aside for her upon his death. Then, the lawyer read further. Bobby did something none of us expected. He gave me half the interest in the diner and the other half to Vanessa! Just like Bobby to be equitable.

Finally, the lawyer read a statement Bobby had handwritten before he died.

The note talked about his guilt for leaving Vanessa but also about his great love for me how Vanessa spent nearly half her life building the diner but it was my creativity that keep it going.

Have you ever heard the term livid before? Well, Vanessa's face turned every shade of livid I've ever seen. I remember sitting there imagining her head filling up like one of those water balloons at the fair and exploding right off her shoulders. Her lawyer patted her hand and told her not to worry. I giggled to myself at the mess of it all. Said my thank yous and goodbyes to his former family and the lawyers and left feeling pretty good, too, considering what had just happened. Financially, I was solid and didn't need to worry about money—for a while anyway.

I closed the diner for three weeks.

When I went back to reopen, there Vanessa stood, waiting outside the door. She offered to buy my interest. I told her I had no intention of selling and offered to buy hers. She fumed at my boldness and told me she'd never sell. Bobby knew I was stubborn as a mule in a blizzard, and he knew his former wife had some of my same shortcomings.

"Well, isn't this a fine mess." Vanessa threw her hands up and when they came down, they landed on her lap as she sat hard against the window's ledge.

"Guess Bobby had the last laugh, huh?" I looked out onto the day with one hand protecting my face from the bright sun. It was early spring then, and the cacti were putting on a show to embarrass the Hanging Gardens of Babylon—gorgeous.

"Since this place is now legally half mine, I want a key." Vanessa was indignant.

"Fine. After José gets here, I'll have him run up to Charlie's to get one copied."

Vanessa let out a small huff and stood back up. "What are we supposed to do now?"

"Well, the diner needs managing. I guess we manage it."

"Together?" She put her hands on her hips.

"What else can we do?"

"It just won't work."

"Why, Vanessa? After all these years, do you still hate me so much?"

"Oh, hell, I could care less about you." She turned away and looked out over the burgeoning desert. "How's this gonna look to the folks around here? Did you ever think about *that*?"

"I just put my husband in the ground. I guess I haven't had too much time to worry about what people are thinking."

"He was my husband too." She scowled when she looked at me. I couldn't very well argue her point and decided by the look of her. Saying nothing was best. Vanessa turned her head away. "Son of a…" She spoke it like a tire going flat.

We looked at each other for a few seconds. I'd been sitting on the planter outside the door across from Vanessa the whole time and my rear end felt numb; so, I stood. Face-to-face with her, it was uncanny how much Vanessa and I looked like each other. She was older, of course, and had severely short, dark copper-colored hair. Her eyes were almond-shaped and emerald green, like mine. She was tall and had some meat to her, like me. Her skin was radiant pink with freckles.

Here, standing in front of me, was the only other woman Bobby had ever loved. We stared into each other's eyes. I can only guess what she was thinking. The scowl on her face was worth a thousand words. Time seemed to stall out and we began to feel ill at ease.

Through it all, a strange feeling welled up deep inside me. For the life of me, I don't know why I did what I did at that particular moment, but I stuck my hand out like I was making a deal.

"So, what d'ya say, partner? Shall we give her a

3

go?" I said it emphasizing my Georgian drawl like an actor in an old western.

And Vanessa did quite the unexpected thing. She grabbed my hand and gave it one hard shake downward.

As we walked together toward the restaurant's door, she shook her head in disbelief and grumbled, "Dear God, help us."

****

Old Spice cologne always makes me think of funerals and vice versa. The scent wafted through our house from my parents' bedroom and down the hallway into mine on the shower's steam. The smell only lasted until I was about eight years old when Momma and Daddy had a huge knock-down-drag-out. Daddy left the house in a snit and drove his station wagon straight into the face of a telephone pole. He was killed instantaneously and left Momma and me all alone.

I was just a young girl when Daddy died. We lived near the historic district in a small town called Milledgeville. On family outings, we'd take horse-drawn carriage rides through lolling, lush gardens, and pass by a dead author's home. We rode the trolley by the Old Governor's Mansion even though we lived close by that were in walking distance. It was Daddy's treat to Momma and me at least once a month. He'd repeat the tale about the history of Milledgeville where he was born and raised and where his momma was born and raised; his momma's momma, hers, and hers the same year Milledgeville was incorporated in 1804. Daddy was just thirty-five when he died. We moved away from lolling hills filled with scented gardens and ended up in the smelly metropolis of Atlanta. Atlanta!

The armpit of Georgia where Mother got job after job in crusty bars serving drinks to strangers…and taking home a few in the process.

For Daddy's interment, Momma had the coroner dress him in his favorite blue seersucker suit, with a cracked pocket watch, and put his cologne on him. I wanted Daddy's pocket watch so bad it hurt, but Momma said it belonged with Daddy. The immediate family members were the only ones who could witness Daddy's body before the closed-casket funeral was to begin. No one smiled during the viewing. People cried and made kind yet insincere comments about how good he looked.

You see, puzzling his face back together had proved a difficult proposition for the mortician. The impact of the car coming in contact with the pole sent Daddy through the window. Safety glass split his head in more than thirty pieces and after mortaring his bones, seaming his skin, and reattaching his hair, the mortician had to reconstruct his nose and chin, after which he layered him unnaturally in a thick application of foundation makeup. It didn't look like Daddy at all. But at least it smelled like him.

That was the first time I ever got to ride in a limousine.

Old Spice and limousines—they remind me of funerals.

Nowadays limos are white instead of morbid black. Limo drivers are still tranquil; still wear a chauffeur's hat, and still help you in and out of the car, but around here the black limo has gone the way of the dinosaur.

That changed shortly after my husband Bobby's death. For the past forty years, I'd been to far too many funerals. Now this.

Sunnydale had lost one of its finest people. Earlier this morning when we pulled up to the graveside, it showed. There were swarms of people. Roberta, Bobby's daughter, said she'd received over fifty bouquets and ten funeral arrangements. Now, what does that say about a person? You must be pretty amazing to have almost the entire town show up for your funeral.

****

I arrived in Sunnydale, Arizona in the heat of the summer. Stepping off the cold bus into the morning warmth made me wither under my thick cover. A bus ride originating the night before in cool mountain air and ending up in the heat of the desert left me peeling off my day-old sweatpants, revealing under them a short summer dress made of thin butter-colored rayon. The inside of my thighs felt dewy.

A bag lady pushing a grocery cart had dropped her coin purse and instinctively, I dropped to my hands and knees to help her collect the quarters, nickels, and dimes, trying to stop them all from skewing off in all directions. I glanced up and noticed a trucker ogling me. I could see him imagining me slipping out of my clothes entirely. He had a look. You know? His tongue maneuvered a toothpick around from one side of his gaping mouth to the other, and he kind of smirked as he watched me. He leaned on the ticket counter and talked to some lackey who worked behind the desk. Now, both men were staring. But only one had a reason.

The smell of diesel hung oily in the air. My long strawberry curls fell over my face when I pulled the gray sweatshirt over my head. I shook my hair back a little. It was then I'd slipped off my sweatpants and it was then both gentlemen stopped talking. I shoved the garments into my backpack, found a stick of cinnamon-flavored gum, and folded it over and over three times with my lips and tongue. It made my mouth water. I walked up to them real smart, chewing my gum. Standing next to them, I could look both men square in the eyes. In Milledgeville, where I grew up, I was one of the bigger girls at school.

I asked "toothpick" if he had a car or something. He bragged about his big rig as if it were wrapped inside his zipper. I giggled because I needed a lift, and it was a *little* funny. The sound of my laughter carried across the room and the echo bounced off bright windows and a cold tile floor. The bus terminal sounded like a big tin drum, and I was aching to end my journey. With just a couple of hundred dollars in my pocket, a forty-five-dollar bus trip would have taxed my savings. A cab was out of the question. This guy seemed like a good prospect. He seemed willing. I only had one hundred miles or so left to get to Phoenix.

I never made it.

After listening endlessly to this yahoo talk about his wife and seven boys, and how he'd never do anything to break up their happy home, we neared a little nowhere spot along a long, dusty highway. I just sat there in my seat with my head propped in one hand while I watched lazily out the window. And while he was unzipping his pants!

I don't know if you've ever been to the Arizona desert, but the heat can melt you. It's a hell of a lot different from the damp, cool air of a coastal town. I watched mesmerizing waves pulse off the desert basin. A landscape of green saguaros, spiny yucca, curly leaf, barrel, and cholla cactus painted the red rock sandstone. I could smell tar-pungent creosote baking under the weight of the sun. It seemed to stick to my skin. I remember yawning at the tranquility of it all.

His droning turned into a nervous chatter and broke me from my spell when he said, "How about a little mouth job." I almost didn't hear him but looked over in his direction involuntarily. He'd pulled out his penis and was massaging it to get it hard.

I screamed.

"Oh, my God. What the *hell* do you think you're doing?"

By then, we were cruising along at about sixty-five when I clamored for the door handle. I don't know what I would have done. Jump? I don't know. Fortunately, I didn't need to jump. When I screamed, he nearly jackknifed his precious Peterbilt when he slammed on his brakes.

The wheezing hydraulics gasped for air in a high pitch wheeze. I thought we were going to crash. Actually, it wasn't because I screamed we nearly crashed. It was because when I saw his dick in his hand, I grabbed my backpack and started thrashing his lap with it. It was only after I turned to see if I could survive a jump from the rolling semi.

No one ever told me how useful a backpack could be. You can keep your valuables in it, carry it around with some modicum of ease, and use it as a weapon if need be.

Well, he reacted like any man would who wanted to protect his penis—he forgot what he was doing. I could see cars reflected in my side mirror slowing behind us as the big truck squirreled from one lane to the next.

The trailer he pulled wagged in and out of sight. Vehicles split off the road behind us. As I clutched my backpack tight, I could feel the outline of the only book I was carrying with me, the Bible. When I looked up again into the mirror and saw those cars peel off onto the roadside, it reminded me of a bad version of Moses in the Old Testament parting the Red Sea.

I held on for dear life to the seat and the dashboard in front of me. We slowed to about forty-five when we careened off the shoulder next to the fast lane. He ended up burying those big truck tires deep into the thick silt of the median. Through the whole thing, his dick was out.

Can you imagine what they would have thought had we crashed and died? Christ. I wanted out. I was only thinking about how to get out.

I unbuckled my belt, held my backpack tight, and jumped from the high seat nearly into the tumbleweed jammed under the front tire. He was tucking his *Johnson* back into his pants and yelling at me like it was my fault—calling me a slut, ugly words and such.

I waved down traffic to let me run cross to the other side and set off on foot. After about five minutes, I heard state patrol cars approaching. They passed me fast coming from the opposite direction en route to the accident behind me. My momma always told me not to hitch rides with strangers. Guess she was right.

I swear I was getting a tan as I walked farther south.

And the shoes I wore when I escaped from the semi weren't shoes meant much for walking. They were espadrilles with a floral design, a yellow matching my summer dress. I'd found them in a Sears catalog at this little gin joint where I served drinks in a dreary, overcast fishing town along the northern California coast. When I saw the pretty model wearing the outfit, I made my decision right then and there to leave for a warmer climate. That's the story of how I arrived in Sunnydale.

****

Fifteen years passed and a lifetime passed with them. During the early spring of 2007, at forty, I buried my only husband.

Bobby was quite a bit older than I was. He was fifty when I walked into his diner, and I was twenty-five. I met him the first day I sauntered into Sunnydale. I didn't feel like catching another ride to some place I'd never been before, and I wanted a glass of lemonade with lots of ice in it like a hot weather person might drink.

My dress clung to me like gauze sticking to a honey jar. Bobby noticed me through the window; he told me a few nights later when we first made love. I fell for him hard, and he returned the favor, something his wife and daughter didn't quite appreciate. Bobby was my first real love. He'll be my last too. I miss him like a child misses hard candy at Christmas time.

His seducing eyes and soft touch make me quiver just to think about. He liked to wash my hair and brush it out after it dried. He treated me like an angel. Bobby used to tell me my skin reminded him of cream-freckled coffee. He said my boobs were too big but he could learn to live with it.

My name changed to Georgette Carlisle. When I arrived here, it was Georgette Daniels. My hair is still long but I keep it pulled back now, and I have crow's feet from the many times I smiled with Bobby.

Our relationship was organic, if you will, like it was meant to be. Although Vanessa, Bobby's ex-wife, tried to stop it, we married soon after their divorce. He left her side the moment he saw me, and I joined his, the moment I saw him.

Vanessa was a good woman. She only did what any other woman who still loved her man would do; she fought to keep him. But there was no keeping Bobby from me. Vanessa knew she'd lost the battle and finally agreed to a divorce.

Bobby moved us into a new house where we made a lovely home. It had a nice big fireplace where we'd camp out in an oversized sleeping bag on cold winter nights, and it's where I still live today.

We'd pull blankets off the bed to cushion the cherry floor under us. We only had one bedroom. The house wasn't big, but it wasn't small. It was perfect for the two of us.

Bobby wanted our place to blend with the desert. He helped place thick, wooden beams over each of the doors and the arbor. The Indians and Mexicans used to build their walls from adobe. Adobe is a mud mixture formed into bricks and baked in the hot sun. It takes on the colors of the earth—warm sienna with hints of rose. There's a lot of clay in the desert earth. The clay creates the rose color you see painted across the land. We built our house with adobe, and together we lived in a pink house. Pink is one of my favorite colors and having an entire house in a pink hue delighted me to no end.

Bobby loved to cook and was good at it too. That's probably why he started the diner in the first place, back when he was still married to Vanessa. It was his passion.

On the back patio of our home, he built himself a barbecue with a brick fire pit where we cooked many dinners. The garden was mine. He helped me rototill a nice big spot, and he built a sturdy wooden fence around it, gave it a coat of honey-colored stain, and we decided we'd grow a vegetable garden there.

Vegetables. I love vegetables. So, in they went! All sorts of seeds—broccoli, cauliflower, radishes, carrots, celery, lettuce, parsley, chard, garlic, green and sweet yellow onions, green beans, snap peas, tomatoes—everything a person needs for a salad and a side dish. Then Bobby built me another box, a special one he made to snap together and taller for potatoes as they grew, rather than using old tires like we used to back home by stacking one ugly tire on another one.

We ate well because of our garden. Bobby built all of it for me. I never imagined life could be so sweet.

After Daddy, through the parade of men Momma brought home, she never once brought home a man like Bobby. I never knew a man like Bobby.

When he died, I was completely alone. Momma had long since passed on during one particularly bad Georgia winter a couple years after I'd moved away to California. Bobby and I didn't have many friends; he was fifty when we met, and I was twenty-five. Well, people my age were a little immature for him, and his friends were a little too mature for me. Plus, I don't think anyone ever approved of us. Still, we never felt lonely because we always had each other.

His daughter Roberta disowned him when he left Vanessa, so our holidays were not spent at big family get-togethers or the way most folks think of spending holidays. We'd still fix huge dinners with our cold crop of root vegetables—sweet potatoes and squash. Our turkey was small but mighty, and always moist. I'd learned from my grandma at a young age how to fix a proper turkey. You always baste every thirty minutes, and you roast it slow and evenly until the last hour when you crank up the heat high to four hundred degrees to brown. My turkeys always turned out moist enough to fall off the bone. The trick is never to cook a turkey with stuffing inside; breading dries it out. You shove citrus fruits inside instead—lemons, tangerines, oranges, limes—anything you can get your hands on. Cut them in half and stuff them inside. Citrus fruits are natural tenderizers because of their acid. I'd slip leaves of sage in between the skin and the breast meat, and butter, lots and lots of butter, slathered inside and outside the bird. Rub salt and pepper hard into the skin, and you'll have the best damn turkey this side of the Mississippi. I'd lay money on it any day of the week and twice on Sunday.

Bobby loved my cooking. He'd come home from the diner and tell me my cooking could outdo his, but he always had nice things to say.

Vanessa cooked for the diner before they divorced.

He handled the business side of things, and she handled the kitchen. When they split, half of the waitstaff quit with her. Bobby had a hell of a time trying to make ends meet. We were building a new home, and the diner seemed like it would fail on more than one occasion. After a couple of years, people forgot about all the nasty gossip and things smoothed out. I was working too. I'd gotten a job at the gas station. It was just down the road in the same strip mall as the diner.

This gas station wasn't your normal gas station. This one had a curio shop with all sorts of knickknacks for people visiting and vacationing in Arizona, specifically Sunnydale. T-shirts touting *I survived Sunnydale, closer to Hell than anywhere!* And *You haven't lived till you've spent the summer in Sunnydale,* funny stuff and desert-themed cups, mugs, forks, spoons, Gold Mine bubble gum, cactus locked inside snow balls, scorpion resin paperweights, little fake saguaro cactus magnets, tiny pots with real 'old man' cactus. All sorts of junk you can pick up easy and give away as mementos of your time spent here.

Since I arrived, I've fallen head over heels in love with Sunnydale. The folks are honest and good, and the earth is real. Bobby and I survived the lean times and built up quite a nice little diner—restaurant, really. After he'd prodded me enough times, I decided to leave the gas station and help him out in the kitchen. Slowly, I started to add recipes of my own to the menu, ones costing less but ones which would still present well. The first new dish I added was fettuccine Alfredo. It included a side salad of organic greens and tomatoes and a chunk of garlic toast. We first served it as a special to see if people would go for it. When we'd sell out night after night, Bobby decided to add it to the menu. It went on like this for years, and for five years now Bobby's has been named *Best of Sunnydale.* People travel north all the way from the big city just to have dinner with us.

I'd worked the diner for going on fifteen years.

Vanessa and Bobby ran Bobby's for thirty years.

Never once, since I'd been with Bobby, had she or her daughter ever come in. Never, until now.

Chapter 2

Two large women working together in a tight kitchen looks a lot like a herd of hips and breasts throwing food around. Mix in one woman who has an attitude and stir in another who cries as uncontrollably as the wind blows—well, it's not a pretty sight at all. We found our newly formed partnership trying.

The first day proved disastrous. Vanessa wanted to do things the way she used to, the way she'd done them over fifteen years ago. I tried as diplomatically as possible to explain we'd changed the menu considerably—no more mashed potatoes and gravy, or creamed hash on toast. We'd updated the fare to suit a finer palate. She didn't appreciate any implication suggesting her food wasn't up to standard and took to pouting, but continued to work, nonetheless. I had to force-feed the new menu down her throat. She spit it back at me like a baby in a highchair.

"What the hell is radic-chee-o?" She said it phonetically—the way it looks. My mistake was correcting her.

"Radicchio. It's pronounced radeekyo." I went on, "It's a purplish-red, leafy kind of vegetable. Sort of looks like cabbage. It can taste mildly bitter but it's great for Italian dishes." I was explaining all about the proper pronunciation and everything a person might want to know about or do with radicchio, on and on. I was chopping up something at the time and didn't pay attention to the offense she'd taken from me telling her all the radicchio facts filling my pea-sized brain. I was just chattering along like a chipmunk after a nut.

"I don't need you telling me how to pronounce words, young lady." Vanessa barked out her objection, untied her apron, threw it onto the counter, and walked off.

"Vanessa, I didn't mean…"

She didn't break her stride and left the kitchen before I could finish my sentence. She went straight for the bathroom, disappeared inside, and slammed the door—hard.

We were prepping for lunch and dinner. We were both trying to work the kitchen, the way we had when we each worked with Bobby. He had always done the rest—host, cashier, supervise the waitstaff and bus people, do the books, marketing, and promotion. Those were Bobby's jobs. The name, "Bobby's," for heaven's sake, represented the brains behind the organization. The diner was all about Bobby. I was just a glorified worker in the back. As the day plodded along, I realized that's all Vanessa ever was during their marriage. A fear gripped me while Vanessa threw her temper tantrum in the john.

"Vanessa! Come here, please." My voice must have sounded a bit panicked because she popped out almost instantly.

She was wiping her nose with her hankie and sniveling.

"What?"

"Have you ever worked the front?"

"That was Bobby's job. Why?"

"We don't have a front person." I looked at her in terror. "Do you think you can handle the front, Vanessa?"

"Are you trying to get me out of the kitchen?"

"Vanessa, I've never worked the front. You've never prepared the new menu. What else can we do?" We looked at each other helplessly.

"Good lord. I haven't run a cash register in more than twenty years!"

"Do you think you could figure it out?"

"Well, I do have this sweet little laptop at home with all the bells and whistles. I even have wideband Internet. I can do almost anything on my computer. I don't see why I can't figure out a silly old cash register." Her defiant demeanor gained momentum as she spoke and filled me with hope. "I just need the operating manual, and I can learn how to run it. Sure. Why not? Can you see people's faces when they see me at the front door? Ha! What a hoot. Yes sir. What will people think now? Ha! This is getting weirder every minute." She giggled and at that, turned, and left.

I laughed aloud for the first time since Bobby died. I shook my head and smiled. We had no idea how bad the night would get.

****

The first phone call came only an hour before the doors opened. Glenda, the head waitress, was down with some grizzly infection which made her sound like she'd gone down on a cactus. Sorry, for my crudeness but, come on. Vanessa and I figured with the three other waiters we could manage. We had José bussing, and if need be, Vanessa could serve some of the tables. Bobby decided long ago he only wanted a restaurant with sixteen tables, and he told me why many times. I used to say to him "Yes, dear." I figured it was better than saying "Shut up." You see, with sixteen tables, only three waiters were necessary. If one couldn't make it, two could definitely handle the room. They'd work a little harder, make a little more money in tips, but could handle the room.

Unfortunately, the second call came a half hour later.

Billy, a sweet, sexy, transient thing with a propensity toward over imbibing, called in drunker than a skunk. She said she'd make it in if she had to, but she might puke on a customer. She laughed. I fired her. This left us desperately short with only one waiter for the grand reopening.

"Vanessa!" I screamed as if I'd cut off my finger. She came running in.

"What is it?"

"Billy just called in drunk. I fired her. We're down to one waiter."

"Have you called anyone else?"

I nodded but shrugged my shoulders because I couldn't find anyone.

"No one's available. What are we going to do? This was supposed to be our big reopening night since Bobby died. What are we gonna do now?" That's when I lost it. I thought I'd been strong up until then. I was proud of how well I was holding up through everything—Bobby's sudden death, the funeral, loneliness, Vanessa getting half the restaurant, all of it. The pressure had built and built to a level I couldn't contain. I just went off. I cried like a baby. I didn't make much sound. My shoulders shook and I caved in.

"Georgette." Vanessa said it in a whisper. "For crying out loud, Georgette, I know this seems bad now."

I stopped momentarily to see if she was joking, but she wasn't. I started to cry audibly.

"Oh, now, now. Look, things will be fine."

"No, they won't. They'll never be fine again. Everything is over. I can't do it. I thought I could, but I just don't think I can."

"Please, Georgette, don't cry. You're going to make me cry. I have to greet people in less than a half hour, and I always look like a lobster when I cry."

Vanessa came over to my side. She held me with one arm around my shoulder and tried to console me. I still couldn't stop crying, but in those few minutes I felt how kind Vanessa could be. Her perfume smelled like jasmine tea. She was petting my head and talking me down. I finally lowered my hands from my face and took in a deep breath.

"I'm sorry, Vanessa. I guess all the stress just got to me."

"You gonna be okay?"

I nodded with not a whole lot of conviction.

"Good. That's good." Then she grabbed me face front and said, "Now, what the hell are we gonna do with only one waiter?" She smiled at me for the first time since I'd known her.

Well, needless to say, every dinner was late coming out and getting to tables. The waiter, José, and Vanessa served tables, bussed, and earned every dime they made opening night. I cooked over seventy dinners. Vanessa was warm and greeted everyone with a smile, and she was a whiz on the cash register. I overheard her proclaim to a customer, "Well, stranger things have happened, I'm sure." As she commented, she patted Mr. Rigger on the back as he was leaving. Mr. Rigger had lived in Sunnydale nearly sixty-five years. He and his wife Bethany frequented the diner often when Vanessa and Bobby were still married. They stopped coming in after the divorce but started back up about seven years ago. I guess they forgave Bobby.

Not once had they spoken to me.

Chapter 3

Going through my husband's belongings was one of the saddest times in my life. Prolonging the advent of this task was my first desire. "Let It Be," the Beatles song, came to mind. "Mother Mary, where are you?" I'd poke my head into his closet and smell his scent. Then, I'd shut the door. Time after time, I'd go through the same thing. Sometimes when the mood hit, Gangster, my cat, and I would sit on the floor and rummage through old pictures, newspaper clippings, and letters he'd mailed to me. Bobby had an endearing peculiarity. Instead of handing me a card or note, he'd mail them to me instead. What a thrilling way to receive someone's love, federally!

On one of those days looking through boxes and memorabilia, I happened upon an old letter handwritten to Bobby with a canceled stamp dated June 1, 1980. Bobby's name and address was written in a pen I would soon come to know well. The letter was from Vanessa. The date was years before we met and married. When I realized what I'd found, a thousand feelings flooded my mind—questions, you know. One question for sure, like *why would he hold onto a letter from his ex-wife for so long?* It wasn't some long-felt proclamation of love or bitter words from a recent argument. The letter was more, how shall I say, informational. She was relaying a story from her childhood, a specific event from long ago. After I read it, the questions weren't resolved in the least. In fact, it created more questions for me. This is what it said:

Dear Bob,

I don't quite get why you care or why you want to know about this, but here you go. When I was only eight years old, Terrence and I talked and threw rocks at a saguaro while Uncle Joe and Father would hunt dove and quail.

"Stay here and don't wander off or you'll get shot!" Father warned us as they disappeared into the brush with rifles at their sides.

The desert didn't offer much shade that day, only a few scraggly mesquites where we could sit if we dared! This wasn't the first time Terrence, and I went out with Father and Uncle Joe. I remember many times during our outings we would have to shoo away a tarantula with a stick or see a rattler slither by. We'd scream ear-piercing shrills, and Father and Uncle Joe would run back to us out of breath. Like I mentioned, I was only eight and Terrence was seven. We were little kids and petrified of the dangers we might find in the desert. While we waited, we would talk and throw rocks.

I remember one time; Father let Terrence hold and aim the gun. After much complaining about it, he let me too. I was a girl and back then, girls weren't supposed to behave like boys—at least, not while parents watched. But I made such a fuss Father finally let me hold and aim it too. Then I did a most unforgivable thing. I pulled the trigger!

When it fired, I fell backward. The kick of the gun was fierce and knocked me on my butt.

Father ripped the gun out of my hands and got in

my face. He screamed at me for shooting it and told me I was never to do it again.

My heart broke because he'd never yelled at me before; Mother was the disciplinarian. She would threaten us with harsher action from Father, which usually never came. This time he pulled me up by one arm, cracked my rear, and told me to go sit in the horse carriage. A few minutes later, Terrence came to sit with me. I was still crying, and he called me a big baby.

"I'm not a big baby! I'm not a big baby!" I jumped down from the carriage and walked up to Father and Uncle Joe. I had my say to Father and turned to walk back to the carriage. My father stopped me by grabbing me by my shoulder. That's the day Father and I had a 'meeting of the minds.' We'll call it that, anyway. That's the day he called me 'young lady.' Back then, most girls might have taken it as a compliment. Not me. I fumed, turned around, and hotfooted it back to Terrence.

I guess I've always been self-assured. A good trait, I guess, when you need it. You have to pick your battles—that's my motto.

Well, Terrence laughed and laughed when I got my butt whipped because he felt Mother and Father normally treated me with kid gloves—his words, not mine. Terrence had always been the one, how shall I say, put to the task! Ha! He'd get a beating at least once a week, usually on the weekends when he'd run off to the watering hole to swim. Not only did he swim but he'd smoke cubebs and drink homemade beer with one of the other boys whose parents used to make the stuff. He'd come home like a man on a night out with the boys. He'd say in his defense, "We was only drinking milk and smoking corn silk, Pa!" But no milk I've ever smelled had a scent like that! He was just a boy too. He hung out with some older kids and even though Mother and Father tried repeatedly to stop it, he'd still meet up with them one way or the other. They all turned out to be perfect gentlemen. They got newspaper jobs, riding bikes door-to-door delivering...and selling, too, for the local rag in Kingman.

That's just one of the many memories I have about Terrence. Hope you enjoy.

Love, Vanessa

As I said, the letter read like it was written to an old school chum, nothing inflammatory, except maybe for poor Terrence. Bobby never mentioned Vanessa's family or his in-laws. The glimpse of Vanessa's brother made me realize how little I knew about her—about how little I knew about many of the people I'd lived with over these years, here in Sunnydale. I guess maybe I always assumed Vanessa's family was all dead, like mine. I guess I never really thought about it. I folded the letter, stuffed it back into its envelope, and put it back into the box.

Chapter 4

Maybe it was a coincidence of wishes when I cursed him. We'd never really had any big fights—I think I mentioned this before—and we'd been married for nearly fifteen years when it finally happened. For the past month, however, Bobby had been edgy and out of sorts. He seemed more forgetful lately, and he kept to himself. We'd just finished with an early Saturday dinner, and I had the lasagna pan soaking. My hands were red from the hot, soapy water I'd used washing dishes and wiping down counters. Bobby pulled out the day's newspaper, opened to the sports page, and covered the entire freshly cleaned table with it. For whatever reason it irked me, and I told him he'd have to wipe off his own ink smudges when he was done reading. He'd been off emotionally and physically, if you get my drift, and seemed to be taking things out on me. For the past month, mind you, I had taken his slight abuses, but tonight I got to the boiling point and popped my lid. After my spiel about recleaning the dinner table, he made some under-the-breath comment I could barely hear.

"What did you just say?"

"Nothing," he grumbled.

"You did say something. Dammit, Bobby, tell me what it was." My voice began to quaver.

"I said, you sound like Vanessa." He buried his

head deeper into the paper.

I threw my washrag at him and it hit him in the back of the head. I was getting teary because we'd not been seeing eye-to-eye for over four weeks. I stormed off and went into the bedroom.

He always talked about Vanessa in the kindest way, but lately I was hearing her name come up more and more, like he missed her or something. We'd talk about going on a road trip and he'd say, "When Van and I were younger, we used to…" Then I'd bring up wanting to go to Phoenix for a night at the symphony, and he'd bring up the fact Vanessa and he used to go to Laughlin to see stage shows there, and in Phoenix, but they always seemed to enjoy the Laughlin shows more. It seemed like every time I said something, he'd get nostalgic about Vanessa.

He missed Roberta terribly. She'd pushed him out of her life after her parents split and after he married me. It broke his heart. Roberta could be very cruel and vindictive. At first, he blamed it on her age and immaturity about married life. After years, however, hearing her snide comments and feeling her rejection, he began to go inside himself. Bobby laid down the law; we weren't allowed to bring up Roberta even in passing, light conversation. Her name was forbidden from our household. Still, we couldn't hide from Roberta's presence within our community.

Roberta had been on the fast track in Sunnydale from the day she finished high school. She left Sunnydale to go to school in Las Vegas. She commuted three days out of the week for two years to go to the community college there. Then, after she transferred to the university, she moved there until she graduated. Her degree was in engineering like her grandpa. She'd scored highest in her class. She cut her long, orange hair into a professional do to better suit her upcoming career. Her new boyfriend was in her graduating class as well, and when she finished college, she moved back in with Vanessa and Bobby. After a year, the boyfriend, Rick, followed her from Vegas to Sunnydale. He proposed and they bought a home here.

Roberta freelanced, and Rick went back and forth from Sunnydale to Bullhead City and Laughlin where he worked during the week. His returns home were always a little tense but after a few hours of reestablishing their relationship, Roberta and he slipped into their usual weekend routine.

It was only a couple of years after; Roberta became civil to her father. Up until then, it was rough going. Even though Bobby acted tough on the outside, I knew his heart was crumbling because of it. He never missed an occasion to send her a card—her birthday, her anniversary, Thanksgiving, Christmas, Valentine's Day, 4th of July—or write her a note to touch base with her. Roberta never reciprocated. She was aloof and cold to her father.

He always blamed Vanessa, and one day he called her on it. Vanessa stood her own and told Bobby he was living a fantasy. She said he needed someone to blame for his own actions, and she was the only person who seemed the reasonable suspect. He flung the phone across the room after talking with her and cried. It was the first time I saw him cry. He couldn't blame anyone but himself. Himself and me.

As time lolled along, he began to feel the longing less. But something seeped into our marriage slowly; it couldn't be seen or felt until it stood like a monolith before us. It just appeared one day, big as life. By then, it was too late. We'd been at odds and hurt and pain tend to breed anger. I was hurting and needed my old Bobby back again. I attempted to reenact things we'd done when we first got together. I bought sexy lingerie and body butter, made candlelight dinners, and read dirty books to him. I'd cook while wearing only an apron with spiked heels and sit on his lap naked. We tried several times to make love, but he couldn't. It was me. Surely, it was me.

The lasagna dinner I fixed night was basic. We were growing apart, and I wanted him to leave, to go away. But if he were to return, he'd have to return like his old self. Those were going to be my terms.

After I threw the washrag at him and stormed out, I came back in to tell him so. But he'd already left.

He sat slumped over the sports page; blood was dripping off the table and pooling by the table leg. His arms hung flaccidly by his sides and there was no sign of Bobby anymore.

The nine-one-one operator told me I had to quit screaming because she couldn't understand what I was saying.

The paramedics had to pull me off of Bobby and proceeded to pump his chest, while they gave him artificial respiration, while they set up the portable paddles, while they shocked him repeatedly, even while they pronounced him dead on the scene at 6:07 p.m.

It's interesting, you know. What's funny was I needed to find out if he wanted to leave. I didn't really want him to leave, not really. My emotions were out of whack. The thought was just that, a thought and nothing more. But, when you're wishing, does the Grantor of Wishes understand this? That the thought was only an impulse, a mental projection, or a petty muffled utterance?

I didn't want him to go. Not really. I didn't want to live without him, and now I wished I had died before, long before, because the idea of living without him was unbearable, unimaginable. My life ended when Bobby died. Was this a coincidence?

Chapter 5

Early spring in the desert isn't like spring in the cool Northwest with tulips bending over a warming earth. Spring in the desert is a quick burst of life and as the heat swells life fades. Early spring is cool in the morning and warm, hot even, in the afternoon. Temperatures can reach close to ninety degrees even at the birth of spring.

Heat baked a jasmine growing on an arbor next to the white tent. Its pink petals steamed under a blanket of warmth and lazily plated the air. Bees flew wildly buzzing their disapproval of people in close proximity. They were so near I could feel the batting of their wings drum against my skin, like a butterfly kiss on your lips. A grackle rocked out a ragged "caw caw caw" to its mate who answered in kind. The bright sun clashed head-on with my mood *du jour*. Just like the desert to fake you out, the oasis just out of reach. Others in attendance glanced at me in a plastic veneer I'd learned to recognize—to live with. Luckily, my hazy veil covered my swollen eyes and red nose. I wore black linen the day of Bobby's funeral. A vague salty film covered my dry tongue when I finally swallowed. Remembering to breathe was my only real responsibility. I just had to survive it.

The cool morning was churning into a hot afternoon by the strike of eleven o'clock. I arrived earlier than Vanessa or Roberta. The reverend greeted me with a pat on the hand and sad, sad eyes. He expressed his sorrow and led me to my seat where I sat alone for a while.

Then Vanessa arrived. Like a dethroned queen with her following. Roberta bumped into my leg when she passed by me to take her seat as a family member alongside the casket. She didn't apologize.

Four chairs lined the gravesite for us. The minister spoke cautiously, sadly, and lifted his head to God with widespread arms.

The Bible sat in front of him on a spindled podium of cold, tarnished steel with a gold ribbon slung between two open pages of silky, thin paper. I could only imagine our Lord Jesus' words in red and everything else written in black. A funeral jury stood behind us, to the sides of us, and in front of us—in judgment. They all stared and expected the worst. But in my opinion, the worst had already happened. Bobby had died.

Upon giving his final prayer, the minister turned to the five men of the honors detail. He nodded for them to proceed, and in doing so, the uniformed men stood erect with rifles quick to their sides. The lead man called out, "Attention! Half left face. Port arms."

"Ready, aim, fire."

"Ready, aim, fire."

"Ready, aim, fire."

"Present arms."

"Half right face."

Taps blew slow and languidly while two of the men lapped and overlapped our country's flag. The mournful wail of the trumpet caught in my throat like a rock—lapping, overlapping, once, once again, then twice. The horn blower soulfully repeated the last song's phrase three times lapping, overlapping, once, once again, then twice until the man finished folding the flag. Red stripes, blue background to white stars all represented in part to the flag now a triangle of folded fabric. After the final note, one man presented me with the flag in commemoration of Bobby and his service to the United States. I heard Roberta make a noise with her tongue, a *tsk*. Vanessa's head was down the whole time and she didn't twitch; I could see her from the corner of my eye.

The presenter took one step back from me and marched back to the others. He then toed and pivoted into line with his men and called out.

"Order arms."

"At ease."

They stood with their legs slightly apart. My heart still pounded in my chest from the sound of the guns. I watched them intently as they took their dutiful places. My face was wet, but I don't remember crying. Yet, I must have.

I had long since been hurt by people omitting my name from their guest lists. Even so, several of our diner's patrons stopped by the house to check on me after the services. Vanessa held a wake at her home in honor of her ex-husband and his family. I wasn't invited. But Vanessa and Roberta couldn't hurt me anymore by leaving me off their party list. My days of mourning had long since begun. Bobby's collapse over the sports page marked the commencement of me grieving.

Chapter 6

Anymore, pulling into my driveway left me with mixed feelings. It had been but less than a month since the funeral, and I still expected to see Bobby at home. It's funny how death works. You forget for moments at a time the person you've lost is gone. You think you can still pick up the phone or call out from the kitchen window to get their attention, and you honestly but briefly believe you'll hear their voice answer back. Then your mind whirls into a vision and you feel an awful pit in your gut, a constant reminder of the day he died—the paramedics trying so desperately to revive him, and then yelling "Clear!" You remember their faces as they looked around at each other, shaking their heads, clocking the time they stopped trying. The newspaper strewn in sections across the floor, the cat rubbing against my leg, my knees cracking against the wood when I lost the strength to stand any longer, and seeing the wet washrag lying on the floor beside the chair.

Then your mind reels in a fast-forward motion to scenes at funerals, Mother's, then Bobby's, imagining the gathering you weren't invited to at Vanessa's—a conjured scene, a comment, a sneer. It all happens so fast like someone hit you with a slingshot because you're still in the car pulling up into the drive when your mind snaps back to reality. It's exhausting.

Instead of seeing Bobby, Gangster went scurrying off with another catch in his mouth. I threw the car into park and jumped out screaming, "Gangster, you stop right now!" He had made his way to the front door and had a baby rabbit in his jaws. "Drop it!" I walked hard in his direction and he did exactly what I instructed him to do.

He was very well trained, almost like a dog.

"Good boy," I told him. You see, baby rabbits are about the size of small rats but they're much cuter. I picked up the poor little thing, but too late as it turns out. By then the bunny was lifeless. "Gangster." I whined his name irritably. But he thought he'd done a good thing, again. He purred loudly as I held the dead little thing in my hands. I'd heard somewhere cats will bring you their kill as a gift. It's their way of saying thank you, and Gangster was a smart cat who could find a nest of anything and steal the babies out of it. So I said, "Thanks, Gangster," grimacing at the gift, and proceeded to go out back by the garden where all the rest of his prey lay dead, under a branchy mesquite or under a pile of dirt, to give the poor thing a proper burial. I hadn't even gotten into the house when I was grabbing the shovel and digging another hole. My life up to this point had become one stream of funeral services. Similar future burials flashed before my eyes. What an unbearable existence it seemed at the moment.

When I finally got inside, dirt covered the knees of my pants, my hands felt gritty, and the cat was following me around like a puppy. He wanted his evening treat. The sound of the electric can opener brought with it a yowling from Gangster and sounded like wild cats chasing a mouse.

"Here ya go, tiger."

He responded with a sexy, breathy yow. Then the only sound in the house was of delicate lapping up of food and the hum of Gangster's purr while he ate his fishy dinner.

My stereo was stocked and ready to go with DVDs of Tony Bennett, K.D. Lang, Satchmo, Danny Kay, Frank Sinatra, and Count Basie—music Bobby had turned me onto. I set a kettle of water on the stove, grabbed the remote control off the counter, and clicked on the music. Unwinding to old-time jazz and sipping chamomile seemed like a beautiful way to relax, a charitable gesture to myself after my first day back at work since Bobby's death. But more importantly, a day back working alongside his ex-wife.

After lounging on the sofa and trying to figure out the day's crossword puzzle, I got up to take a bath and wash off the day. In the shower, I started to get riled and angry—at what, I wasn't sure. Then it dawned on me. Bobby had left me. In this one flash, all I wanted was to get into bed and stay there under my blanket, hide away. Then, a sound rumbled out of me from the core of my gut and it felt like it was wrenching out my soul with it—a guttural wailing echo against the hard glass and mirror of the bathroom hitting the water and cascading onto the tile floor. A roar from a snared beast caught in a trap. I yelled with all my pain, all my fury, and kept repeating, as if each convulsing sob freed me from the torment. Bending forward in agony, steaming water ran over my face. My voice strained out a final howl and I lost my breath. I panicked. I sucked in air. When I did, I sucked in water too. Trying to swallow, I spat and gagged. My hands plastered flat against the shower's stall, and I struggled to keep from falling.

I slumped onto the hard, warm tile. My butt landed on a broken piece of slate and I felt my skin break. I rolled off the shard and laid on the shower's floor crying. For how long, I don't even know. I wanted to disappear but leaving wasn't an option. Anyway, I couldn't run away from my anguish. I couldn't leave. The restaurant would fold, and then I became angrier with Bobby.

How could he do this? How could he just up and die on me? He hadn't told me he was sick. What was it exactly the doctors said about him being ill? What did they say about nearly three years before?

Nothing would ever be the same.

I sank in between the cool sheets with my cat curled against my side and fell asleep.

Chapter 7

"Hello, Mayor, Mrs. Pyle. How you doing this fine Sunday?" Though I tried to mask my Georgian drawl, the *fine* still sounded a little like *fan*. I was walking Gangster on his leash down the sidewalk in front of the Church of Christ. Services had just let out and everyone looked enlightened and full o' smiles and kindness as they clamored around the front of the church entrance. Older folks and children wore their best Sunday clothes while teenagers sported hip-huggers, tight T-shirts, metal in their faces, and dark eyeliner making them look more like Satan worshipers than Christians. But there they were, pouring out of the church's pious mouth onto its holy steps.

"Why, we couldn't be better if the Lord reached down and touched us on our heads, right, Helen?" The mayor said it loud so everyone could hear him.

Mayor Harold Pyle seemed more like a caricature than a real person, and he seemed to accentuate those parts (physical and verbal) already exacerbated. The disproportion of his large forehead accentuated his pea-sized eyes—eyes darting all too frequently as he conversed. He had an oily, beak-shaped nose with deep pores covering the end of it and appearing as tiny black dots. Just when I was concentrating on his nose, he pulled out a hanky and dabbed his snout, rubbing up to his forehead, and down around the rest of his greasy face. His experience in church must have gotten his follicles pumping.

Although he wasn't from Arizona, in fact, he was from somewhere in the Midwest. He tried to put on a southwest accent, like a cowboy. Helen Pyle smiled weakly and nodded in agreement with her husband.

"Oh, but the Lord did just bless us, didn't he?" Pyle flipped his head back in the direction of the church and the church folk and gave a big belly laugh. "See you next Sunday, Pastor! Bye all!"

The mayor never only talked to one person; he kept a stage close at hand. I was simply the conduit facilitating a lead-in for his next line. As he left his audience, he waved at everyone, but tipped his hat in my direction, made a smooching sound in the direction of Gangster, took hold of Helen's elbow, and led her away. She made dainty, quick steps as if he was pushing her too fast.

I'd only spoken with the mayor a few times when he would happen into the diner to get lunch. He seemed pleasant enough but would talk so loudly the customers would stop eating and look up. They couldn't help but listen to him. It seemed odd to me so much volume could come out of such thin lips.

I've always said Sunnydale has only two seasons—spring and summer. I've always held there are only two temperatures—warm, and hotter than hell. We only get a couple of days of cool weather compared to other parts of the country, or what others might think of as cool. Very seldom do temperatures here dip below the freezing point, and only in early winter mornings. On those cooler days people don coats or sweaters, yet Mayor Pyle always wore a jacket, and it seemed he only had two. One was a bright yellow and brown tweed jacket he wore with a matching yellow tie. It looked as though when he bought it, the tie was already pinned to the lapel. The other jacket was a bright turquoise polyester number with double stitching he seemed to always wear for public speaking engagements. To coordinate the turquoise jacket, he'd wear a western hat and decorate his face in stripes like the traditional Mohave Indian by finger painting stripes on his cheeks and forehead. He thought it gave him an authentic "look of the people." Poor Mayor Pyle didn't have a lot of hair, so he went in annually to some surgeon who flayed open his scalp and inserted plugs of hair along each cut. Every year he'd have four new lines put in because his own follicles never produced new hair around the incisions, his scalp looked like a quilting of tiny X's where the plugs had been introduced. Everyone knew about it. Talk about someone getting hair plugs is hard to keep quiet, especially in a small town.

Pyle was a slight man, and his wife was even slighter. You rarely ever saw them together except at church and during elections when he had to show a unified front. But if plain had a name, its name would be Mrs. Helen Pyle. I know this sounds mean, but she blended into a crowd. For instance, if there were three people and you were asked to tell who those three were, you'd remember two and forget Mrs. Pyle. Unless, of course, you remembered this great big bag she always carried around with her—a floral crackled leather tote. It seemed so out of character for Helen to lug it around all day. She looked put-together otherwise. But the tote stood out. Helen donned it proudly. I always felt the urge to yank it off her arm, run into a locked room, and rummage through it like a girl with her mother's purse. Helen was versions of black and white, gray, and lighter gray, beige and cream. Helen was vanilla ice cream and she always carried this bright swanky purse around—with its impressionistic green leaves, red petals, and yellow stamens—like a raspberry molasses topping for ice cream sundae.

Of course, the mayor was no movie star himself. He had a degree from an offshore college in business administration and served as a city manager for a few months some two thousand miles northeast in a larger city. It was this experience he flouted to get elected here to the esteemed position of mayor. They had bought a motor home and set off to see every state in the union. They ended up in Sunnydale.

Mayor Pyle seemed genuinely interested in issues of the town. Every once in a while, he'd just sit in the restaurant and stare. He'd come in late for lunch, just after the shift ended, and linger until just before we started setting tables for dinner. He'd slug down a few beers then head home. But while he ate, he would gaze out the window. Maybe he envisioned a crane rebuilding our little town into a larger metropolis. Sometimes he'd wipe at his eyes and nose, sitting there thinking and staring. Maybe he was sad, sad he'd settled for a small-town life, at the lack of grandeur being a mayor in Sunnydale. Anyway, it seemed he longed for something more. He was one of those kinds of people who appear to look at you but are really far away and spinning forever inward, thinking of who knows what, but definitely not listening to you. After he finished speaking with you, he'd say, "Good, good.

Nice talking with you. Keep up the good work." Those words meant zero in relation to your discussion with him and easily slipped off the surface into a flotsam of any meaningless conversation. When the mayor spoke, he was just like the rest of the politicians—he never committed to anything but himself and talked about everything.

I remember he'd driven up to the diner one particular day not long after Bobby died. It was late and I was just about ready to go home for my midday break. He stopped me before I could get into my car.

"Georgette!" He rolled down his window to yell out.

"Hello, Mayor."

"Georgette, may I have a minute of your time?" He was getting out of his car and was smoothing down his hair flat onto his head. It looked shiny when the sun hit it, and a tiny line of sweat beads appeared across his oversized forehead. He pulled out his hanky and patted down his face.

"Sure. What's up?"

"How long you been running this here lovely diner, Georgette?"

"Hmm. About fifteen, sixteen years, I guess. Why you asking, Mayor?"

"Have you ever thought about just selling, getting out of it? You know, take off and relax? This place makes good money, doesn't it? I'm sure you've built up quite a healthy nest egg. What, with Bobby's inheritance and all." I had a mind to think the good mayor was prying. But I don't believe his conversation was about that.

"It pays the bills and keeps people employed,

Mayor." I didn't know where he was going with the sudden questioning, a questioning which felt a lot like an interrogation.

"How's it going with you and the *missus*?" He said it like a dirty word.

"Vanessa? Oh, fine, I suppose. We're still working out a few bumps. Why all the questions, Mayor?"

"Oh, just my own curiosity more than anything, I s'pose. Hey, can I still get something cool to drink and a bite?"

"Anything for you, Mayor. Just tell 'em I saw you outside and it's okay by me." I unlocked my door and got into the car. Its interior sweltered from sitting under the unforgiving sun and you could smell the upholstery, it was so hot. I sat for a second while I flipped on the air to the maximum level and rolled down all the windows to help blow the heat out. My car door was still open when the mayor got to the diner's entrance. I was fumbling around with the keys, buttons, and the visor when I briefly looked up at him. At the same moment he turned back to look at me. He glared. When he realized I'd seen him, he turned his sneer into a pressed smile, tipped his hat to me, and yelled, "It's damn hot today, isn't it?"

And he walked inside.

Looking back, the wheels must have been churning quite a while before then.

Chapter 8

Helen grew up in the highbrow part of Stratford where she was raised a proper lady by her old Aunt Birdsey, who had married into Weller Lumber wealth when she was only seventeen. She helped seed a path to Helen's interest in culture—the arts and literature, especially the writings of Flannery O'Connor. Birdsey, originally from Macon, delivered tale after tale of the sweaty southern coastal towns of Georgia. Her family migrated to the New England states when she was just about to enter high school. She fit into the stuffy society of Connecticut like a square peg in a round hole. With a drawl reminiscent of the place she was raised, her schoolmates chided her and laughed when she spoke. But at her coming out party, she was luminescent. Her southern belle upbringing had served her well. She walked fashionably late down a curvy staircase like Scarlet O'Hara in *Gone with the Wind*.

Birdsey had caught the eye of a wealthy miller's son, Joseph, who was a big, ruggedly handsome boy who played football for the school team. The couple became the most enchanting item, and this propelled Birdsey into the rarified air of the popular student and homecoming queen status. They married as high school sweethearts. But try as they might, they couldn't raise the large family each had hoped for. Miscarriage after miscarriage left Birdsey's reproductive system shredded and after much persuading by doctors, the two stopped trying.

At age eleven, Helen's parents were both killed while on a cruise through the Caribbean, leaving Aunt Birdsey at the helm of her niece's guardianship.

Birdsey and Helen seemed destined soul mates. After grueling games of croquet, Birdsey and Helen would dine out in Birdsey's meandering English-style garden where they sipped spiced tea with mint sprigs.

Because she missed the gardens of Georgia, Birdsey planted flowering fruit trees, built gazebos, and put in cobbled walks threaded with moss and creeping jenny, alyssum, and lobelia. Her favorite plant, however, was fuchsia and she hung vast varieties from painted pergolas and wooden arches. After each growing season in the fall, she would pull out each fuchsia from its hanger and plant them in the ground. By her fifth year, she had grown an entire garden of fuchsia reaching nearly twenty feet high. One year, Birdsey felt the garden was getting unruly and she climbed a ladder herself to tie the tips of opposing plants together in an arch, which made the place feel like a secluded covered path. Birdsey hired workers to set down thick slabs of green China slate steppingstones through the archway. Then she added concrete benches so a person could sit beneath the tumult of pendulous fuchsia flowers.

When Helen was a teenager, Birdsey and she used to sit in their special garden with tea and read books together. Birdsey was thrilled to have another female in the house, and Helen was her confidante. It was upon Birdsey's urging Helen became interested in writing. Birdsey arranged for private tutors and sent her to New

York for further schooling. When Helen decided to go to college, Birdsey sent her to Dartmouth.

Dartmouth was where Helen met Harold Pyle. His slick style attracted her attention. She'd never met anyone like him. The gentlemen in the families around Stratford were country club reared and knew all the right words—they never acted out of manner. Harold was different. Fun, daring, and loud. He winked at Helen and called her "girly girl." He overdid. His carriage was slanted and cocky. His clothes bagged in all the wrong places. Harold's eyes were closely set. The hat he wore reminded Helen of a mobster's hat and the oversized padding in his jacket made him look like a trapezoid triangle. His spats were never the right match for his suit, but it didn't matter. Helen swooned in his company.

It was only after they'd been married Helen began to realize her mistake. Harold couldn't hold down a job; he played cards until all hours of the morning with the boys; he drank heavily on occasion and came home with the smell of another woman on him several times. By then, Helen and Harold lived in Chicago and were planning to move again to the slow town of Ames, Iowa. Harold's eye was on a move into the world of politics. He thought his smooth-talking ways fit perfectly with a career in civil service. When he failed at the county level there, the Pyle's decided to make one more move out west, finally ending up in Arizona. After holding several odd jobs and Helen's refusal to make yet another move, Harold ran for mayor of Sunnydale after the incumbent announced his retirement as a public servant. As the sole contender for the position, Harold got the job.

Chapter 9

When Roberta walked in, the restaurant was buzzing with people talking, eating, and rushing to get back to work. Today's lunch special was grilled pork set in a roasted tomatillo sauce and barbequed baby Yukon gold potatoes on the skewer. The lunch fare's fragrance was tantalizing and permeated the restaurant, spilling out onto the sidewalk and down the strip. Each time a customer walked in they would tell Vanessa how good it smelled. But when Roberta walked through the doors, Vanessa got quite a different greeting from her daughter. Her face was pinched and set into a scowl. She stood by her mother while Vanessa cashed out the party leaving.

"Hi, honey. Want some lunch?" Vanessa beamed at her daughter. But Roberta's face remained hard. She didn't say anything, and so I decided it was better to leave them alone.

"She acts like she owns the place!" Roberta huffed quietly.

"Well, she does, Roberta." Vanessa kept counting her till.

"Not all of it. That's how she acts." Her scowl accentuated her words.

"She owns half, Roberta. I think it gives her the right to act the part, don't you?"

"She's a bitch."

"Christ, Roberta. What's eating you today? Keep your voice down."

Roberta huffed and set her purse on the counter.

"Aren't you supposed to be at work?" It was a Wednesday—the middle of the week.

"I took the day off." Roberta fidgeted inside her purse and then pushed it forward nearer the cash register. "I heard a big corporation is looking to buy some land around Sunnydale. They want to put in a fancy tourist attraction along this corridor. Right here too."

"What are you talking about? I haven't heard anything."

"That's because you hide your head in the sand. You don't watch TV, you don't read the local paper, and you never go out! You do a great impersonation of an ostrich, Mother." Her face looked accusatory.

Vanessa reacted in her own defense. "TV is all commercials, sex, and violence; and the newspaper here is like a high school paper. Anyway, why are you picking on me all of the sudden? Get off my back, Roberta. Talk to me like an adult or else leave."

"I just heard something about the land and wondered if you had heard anything."

"No. I haven't. And until I hear otherwise, I'll just believe it's some rumor. Now, I'm busy. Go for a walk or something, Roberta. I can't believe you took the day off to talk to me about this." Vanessa's voice rose and sounded more like a question than a comment.

Roberta pulled at her purse, grabbed a folding mirror out of it, and checked her face. She wiped at the corner of her mouth and coughed slightly. She closed the mirror and slipped it into the zippered compartment of her handbag. Roberta looked solemnly into her mother's eyes. "Rick and I are splitting."

"What?"

"He told me last week when he handed me separation papers and a property settlement. I just left the lawyer's office. His office is close, and I thought I'd stop by."

"Oh, honey. I'm so sorry."

"Yeah. Me too."

"Why didn't you say something before?"

"I don't know. Oh, Mom, I feel just awful. I want to die." Roberta began to get emotional.

I walked in, and Vanessa and Roberta were locked in a meaningful hug. Roberta broke from her mother's embrace when she saw me and turned away. From behind her, I could see she was wiping her eyes. With her back to me, she grabbed her purse, quietly said goodbye to her mother, and walked out of the diner. Vanessa turned and saw me standing there.

"Oh, sorry, Vanessa. I didn't realize."

"What? You didn't realize what?" She said it as though she were pissed at me. She pressed a couple of buttons on the key in the cash register; it made a ding and opened up.

"I'm just sorry, that's all."

"You know, Georgette, it's funny how history repeats itself especially within a family. Bobby left me, and now Rick is leaving Roberta. I don't know why I didn't see it coming. I guess I just hope somehow things will end up differently, you know? Like when Bobby started fooling around with you. I thought it was a silly phase or something. I never believed all these many years later I would be alone. I wonder sometimes

49

if you'd never come here at all if things would have worked out the same way. Probably not."

I didn't know what to say. We were at work, the restaurant was packed, and we were having this muffled conversation by the register. I began to feel smaller and smaller. I was disappearing in clear view. I just stood there and let her have her say. Inside, I knew I'd been waiting for this moment for years. I thought I could stave off the moment longer somehow. But here we were, talking face-to-face about the plaid elephant in front of us, how I stole Bobby away from her. Vanessa seemed so much bigger now, stronger, and righteous. I felt like a used shoe. It wasn't over yet.

"You walk around here like you've done nothing wrong." She was picking up momentum and feeling good about finally letting everything out. "But, in fact, you ruined my family, split us up! You took everything away from Roberta and me. Now, here we finally stand discussing it. But for what purpose? None. Nothing. It doesn't mean one damn thing. You know, Georgette, I have a mind to walk out of here and let you know how it feels to be left entirely alone. Maybe I'll sell my half of the diner to someone else. I'm sick of this place anyway—sick of the work, the long hours, and honestly, Georgette, I'm sick of you!" Vanessa slammed the cash register door.

Customers stared. I just stood there with nothing to say, feeling like every eye in the joint was on me, expecting us to resort to fisticuffs. She looked at me with hatred one I knew had started growing in her a long time ago. What could I do? Bobby was the only man I'd ever loved and the only man Vanessa had ever loved. When I didn't respond, she looked at me with disdain, shook her head, and quietly said, "Please." It was like she wanted nothing more than to be hundreds of miles away from me. It was an hour since our lunch shift had started and she walked out.

****

After the rush was over and the waitstaff left, I grabbed one of the open bottles of red wine. I poured it into a tumbler and sat down on the floor. The wine went straight to my head. I hadn't eaten since earlier in the morning but the cabernet felt warm when it hit my stomach and I didn't care after a few more swallows. With no dinner, I would take a small holiday. Granted, it was only for a few hours but still, the unwinding would do me good, and it did.

When I got home, the cat was yowling as if I'd left him with no food for days. I usually returned home from the diner after lunch around two thirty in the afternoon. It was close to dinnertime and Gangster was having a fit, but the cemetery had called to me. I needed to talk to Bobby again. It had been several days since I'd gone there, and I felt guilty.

As soon as I got to his grave, I sat on the ground and began to cry. I still had a full glass of wine I'd taken from the restaurant, and Lord forgive me, I had driven with it. Albeit, only a mile, but still it was illegal.

The rug of grass was still short and green and smelled like a freshly mown carpet. The heat steamed low along the top of it and I kicked my shoes off to rub my feet in its carpet.

"Hey, Bobby. I sure do miss you. Things aren't going so good right now, but I guess you can see that!" I couldn't hold back my tears and had no tissue to wipe my nose, so I used my shirtsleeve. "Your family hates me so much. I understand why, but it still hurts, you know? Why'd you have to leave so soon honey? There's not a day that goes by I don't think about you, about us. Things were good and now I have nothing." I took a long, slow sip from my glass. "You are my only friend, I have no one else. You were the only real family I ever had, ever. When Momma died, I was totally alone. It's not like she and I were exactly close, not after I was grown anyway—that's why I left. Then, when I found you, I found my only true family. So, you see, now I have nothing."

For two hours I stayed there just sitting and sipping my wine, wiping my nose, and feeling sorry for myself. Two hours came and went and not one other solitary soul was there besides me—no landscapers, visitors, preachers, mourners, no one. It was a sad place.

After two hours, I thought about leaving, getting out of Sunnydale once and for all. My plan was to sell my half of the restaurant to Vanessa, or Roberta, or both. I had no one there anymore who meant anything to me.

Maybe I could find a place where people wanted to become friends, close friends, maybe even so close they might consider me part of their family. I was going to set off on a quest in hopes of finding what I'd always longed for as a child—lots of people milling around the table on Thanksgiving, piles and piles of toys at Christmas time, family reunions, fifty-year anniversaries with parents, things I'd only experienced as a very young child and now could barely remember. By Bobby's grave I formulated how I would do all of this. I'd have to find a brand-new location, maybe near water again, sell my interest in the business, sell the house, pack up the cat, get a mover, and disappear. It would be the noblest thing to do. I was not only reminded daily at the diner of Bobby, but I reminded Vanessa about Bobby daily as well. It was the right thing. I knew then what I had to do.

Chapter 10

Even though the world had successfully entered the twenty-first century, Helen Pyle still wore clothes reminiscent of the 1950s—cotton, tight-waisted, button-down dresses with flared skirts. She kept her hair neatly sprayed, tightly twisted, and pinned to the back of her head. Her horn-rimmed glasses added to the flavor of the time. She kept to herself, for the most part.

As the days neared summer, one warm spring afternoon, while the mayor was in Phoenix on business, Helen walked into the diner for lunch and ended up staying for dinner. It was a night we didn't serve dinner, but later in the evening we fixed her some anyway. It was the least we could do.

I'd only seen her with her husband or alone at the mercantile, so this night stood out for me, and Vanessa too. She wore her usual throwback outfit and entered the restaurant pulling off her sunglasses. Few people were still around when she walked in. Aside from two other tables, she had most of the place to herself. She ordered a patty melt and onion rings, which she loved but rarely ate because the mayor said it caused her to have bad breath and she didn't like it. She started out with a coke and by the end of lunch was on her second glass of wine.

Because so few people were there, Vanessa was kind enough to sit with her off and on and talk to her a little between working. Then, everyone but Helen was gone, and she was getting a little tipsy. She'd been there for two hours and didn't appear to be leaving anytime soon. The husband was away, and she was relishing her time alone. I'd always felt sorry for Mrs. Pyle. She seemed nice enough, but she never got a word in edgewise when the mayor was around. She was a backdrop to him.

The giggling started after her second glass of white zinfandel and, after the lunch hour Vanessa poured herself a glass of chardonnay and sidled up to the booth across from her.

The kitchen was nearly clean when José poked his head in and whispered, "You really have to see what's going on out there." He sniggered a little, shook his head, and headed out the back to work in his garden before going home. As he walked out, he said something in Spanish and chuckled a little louder just before pushing through the door.

I untied the back of my apron, hung it from a hook, and peeked out the kitchen door window. From my vantage point, it looked like the girls were ripping it up. Helen's hands were waving, and she was belly laughing. Vanessa's head was dropping, and her shoulders were shaking from laughter. I couldn't imagine the conversation and boldly went out to see what the hell was going on. Helen's tight bun looked loose, and strands of hair poked out of her bun in wisps around her wine-reddened cheeks. Her eyes took on a sexy glaze and sparkled as she spoke.

"Ladies." When I said it, they busted up. "Having some fun, are we?"

"Georgie, sit down. Helen and I were sharing a

glass of wine. Care to join us?"

"Why not?"

"Why not, indeed!" Helen roared when she repeated my statement.

"I'll get some cab; I'm a red wine woman myself." When I got back to the table with my glass, I had to make a decision where to sit. I could sit with Helen, but I really didn't know her, or I could sit with Vanessa. I turned to get one of the other chairs at another table behind me but heard a thick slap on the booth's seat. It was Vanessa's hand. She scooted over and motioned for me with her patting hand to sit next to her.

"Georgie, Mrs. Pyle was telling…"

"Helen, please." Mrs. Pyle untied the silk scarf around her neck and used it like a fan.

"Helen was telling me about how she and Mayor Pyle met."

"Well, he wasn't a mayor when we met!" The wine had loosened her vocal cords and she inadvertently yelled what normally would have been a comment, then giggled and snorted about the volume. Placing her hand over her lips, she went on, "He was the skinniest little nerd in high school!" She pursed her lips and blew out when she laughed like a balloon losing its air. We all began laughing, in part because she was openly getting intoxicated, but also because we were having fun at the expense of the mayor.

Then she asked as she looked back and forth at both of us, "How did you all meet your husband?" She roared at her own boldness. Vanessa looked down at the table and my hands automatically flew up to cover my face. I couldn't believe she'd spoken the unspeakable. It was hysterical. I wanted to bellow out but knew it was inappropriate. Helen remained quiet as she watched us. I sat motionless for a couple of beats when I heard a slow, deep "huh, huh, huh" from the left of me where Vanessa was sitting. I lifted my left hand from over my eye and saw Vanessa outwardly amused by Helen's comments. Then, my hands dropped to the table and we all looked at each other and busted up.

We laughed and talked for quite some time. It turned out the mayor was quite a control freak and she was thrilled he'd left town if only for the next three days. Vanessa and I made it a point to try to arrange a get-together again, just the three of us before his return. We decided after dinner the next night we would go out to Harvey's, our local corner bar, and attempt to sing karaoke. Why not, right?

The sun was dipping in the sky and we were all a little hungry, so we made something to eat. We wined and dined Helen and she had a ball; we all had a ball. It was the first time since Bobby died I hadn't thought of him on the hour. I spent my first night out without my husband in a long time. Helen and I had a girls' night out and enjoyed ourselves.

Chapter 11

"Leyla! I need the purchase agreements for the Sunnydale land ASAP!" Leyla ran into Zach Pinzer's office holding legal documents in front of her ready to put on his desk.

"Sorry, Mr. Pinzer. I just finished making the changes you needed."

"I'll get these signed." He quickly signed the papers as he was talking. "You notarize them and get them off with the seller's copy to the mayor of Sunnydale today. We need this turned around no later than tomorrow. Courier them to him today. Give him all the appropriate mailing packages he'll need to get them back to us. He's waiting for this stuff right now. I just talked to him. So, go! Let me know when he gets it." Leyla ran out of the office with the documents in hand. Pinzer was known around the office as a hard-hitting, hungry, young executive with nerves of steel and a cutthroat style if anything stood in his way.

On the way down to the copier, Leyla nearly ran headfirst into Mr. Chariot. Mr. John Chariot had started Chariot International, Incorporated when he was a young man out of college. With his family's help, he financed his first development project and sold it for enough to pay back his debt with interest, as well as pay staff and laborers, plus make a healthy profit. After twenty-five years, he'd built a reputation as a stand-up person and an honest businessman. He lived by the motto, "You only have your name." And he meant it. He wanted people to associate his name, his company, with respect and decency.

"Leyla, slow down. What's the rush?"

"Oh, I'm so sorry, Mr. Chariot! I'm so sorry."

"What are you in such a hurry about? People shouldn't have to run through the office to get their work done. You tell Pinzer that's straight from me."

"It's the Sunnydale purchase agreements. I have to get them to the mayor today so he can return them tomorrow."

"Did you say Sunnydale?"

"Yes, Mr. Chariot. Mr. Pinzer told me to get them out right away."

"Can I have a look at those, Leyla?" Reluctantly, Leyla handed John Chariot the contracts. He flipped through a couple of pages while they stood together.

"You know what, there's one other thing we might need to specify. I'll take these to Zach right now. You slow down and take a break, okay? This can wait."

"Yes, Mr. Chariot."

John Chariot ventured up to the third floor only on Tuesdays. Normally, he spent Mondays in one of his two satellite offices or at a development site. He closed Zach's office door behind him.

"Zach, what the hell is this? I thought we were clear on corridor properties. No corridors, no tourist traps. I told you Sunnydale is not the kind of property Chariot is interested in pursuing. What do you think you're pulling?"

"John, I've seen it done so many times and very successfully. This is my budget and my baby."

"This is my business!"

"John—"

"It's over, Zach. Find a property with an already established demographic. I don't want to see this sort of formula within our company. Am I clear?"

"But John."

"Am I clear?"

"Yes, sir. You're clear."

After Chariot left, Pinzer sulked in his office. He called the mayor of Sunnydale to tell him about the delay. "Mayor Pyle, hello, Zach Pinzer here. There's been a delay. No, nothing serious. Yes, that's why I'm calling. Is tomorrow okay for you? I'll hand-deliver them myself. Great, see you then."

When Pinzer hung up, he felt stronger and even more sure his plan would work. He'd have to lay low and move quickly. But he'd see this project through. It would be successful. He would be seen as the future of Chariot. Zach stood up behind his desk and stretched. He looked out on the smog blanketing Phoenix.

"Leyla." He called over the intercom.

"Yes, Mr. Pinzer."

"Come in here, please."

Leyla opened the door diminutively. She started to explain how Chariot intercepted her and got the documents, but Zach hushed her.

"Come in and shut the door. Put the 'Do Not Disturb' sign up, too, please." Leyla smiled sweetly. "Are you wearing any underwear today, Leyla?" Leyla giggled and coyly pulled up her skirt around her bare hips.

"Excellent. Come here."

Chapter 12

The southwest sun was doing its usual thing and another warmer than normal spring brought an early onset of cactus flowers. The frying blaze burnt them off before the week was over. Sweat rolled from under my breasts and the bandana around my neck was soaked.

It was about ten in the morning and I still had a headache from all the wine I'd drunk the evening before. Vanessa and I were prepping for dinner when he showed up at the back door, the delivery door. It was ajar to help circulate in some fresh air. This morning that's where he showed up, quite suddenly, as a matter of fact. When I think back, I still can't remember hearing him arrive in a car.

He looked to be in his late twenties, maybe early thirties. He was a young version of a corporate bigwig with his overly-pressed shirt and pleated pants. The only thing out of place was a loosened tie. It looked like he had pulled on it slightly for effect. His nutty-colored, severely short hair glistened with gel.

"Ms. Georgette Carlisle?" He called from the frame of the door.

"That's me."

"Yes, ma'am. If I could have a minute of your time."

"Are you selling something?"

"No ma'am, not sellin'." The left side of his mouth

twitched like he was holding back a smile as he repeated the word just like I'd said it. He cleared his throat by putting a fist up to his mouth. "I need to go over this paperwork with you."

"Paperwork?" I wiped chicken fat off my hands onto the front of my apron, and I walked over to him as I tried to smooth back the hair from my face.

"My name is Pinzer, ma'am." He held out his hand. "Zach Pinzer." We connected hands. His grip was weak like he was afraid he might hurt me. I still grabbed his hand strongly and gave him a solid shake. He must have felt the oil of the fat on my hands. He looked at his shaking hand, grabbed a kerchief out of his pocket, and wiped it off.

"Oh, sorry. I'm cutting up chicken. Preparing for our evening meals, you know."

He had a look on his face like he'd eaten a fly. Then, he folded and stuffed the kerchief back into his pocket and continued his pitch.

"I represent Chariot International Incorporated."

"What's Chariot International Incorporated?"

"Well, we're a conglomerate corporation who has holdings in many areas. Honestly, we've been watching you."

"Watching me what?"

"Your business, ma'am. We've been watching your business. This business has grown from a small interest to what it is today." He smiled like I should be happy about what he was telling me. "And we think this business would fit well into our corporate strategy. You see, we build small boutique malls. Each mall has one focal point restaurant. We believe this little strip mall here could be redone and rebuilt to be a fabulous tourist boutique setting. Kind of like a second Sedona, if you will. All we need is for you to sign our letter of intent to start the wheels in motion…"

"What are you saying?" During his pitch, I felt like I was dog paddling—I didn't know how to respond.

"Chariot International wants to locate along this strip mall, specifically this building. Chariot wants your business. We're offering to buy it for a very generous amount."

Vanessa had been listening while she prepped potatoes. She hadn't missed a beat. I could hear the whooshing strokes from her peeling in the background until. The whooshing stopped when she inserted herself in the conversation.

"Excuse me, young man, but this business is not for sale." Vanessa walked up next to me. Her face was hard. "Chariot International's contract only states a Georgette Carlisle as the primary. I can only discuss this with her."

"Well, I'm Vanessa Carlisle and I own half of this business. I can speak to this subject as well." She took a meaningful breath, "And, young man, your contract," she said it like a dirty word, "is incorrect; this business is not for sale!" She was brilliant. While I was still standing there dumbfounded.

"Excuse me, ma'am, but do you have an interest in Bobby's Diner?"

"Yes, she does. She owns fifty percent and has a say in every aspect of this business too."

"Well, then—" He flipped to a page in the document. "Wouldn't you both like to know what Chariot is offering?" He'd lost his smirk. Vanessa walked right up to him and backed him out the door. He was now standing on the delivery ramp. He looked surprised. She grabbed hold of the doorknob and started to close it. Pinzer yelled the offer just before the door slammed shut.

"Two and a half million!" We could hear his muffled voice continuing outside the closed door. "That's over a million each!" We looked at each other with high brows when he finished.

"I forgot about this…this part of the business." Vanessa headed back to her potatoes.

I stared like a virgin at Vanessa. "What just happened, Van?"

"Some dimwit just tried to buy our restaurant." She giggled slightly and wiped sweat from her upper lip. I put my hand to my mouth and laughed out loud just once.

"Come on, Georgie, we have a business to run. Yuppies make me sick!" By then it was just before dinner and we were still talking about it. Vanessa untied her apron and threw it onto a counter. "This sort of thing used to happen all the time back when me and Bobby ran the place. The bastards think they can bring their big business mentality into our little community and give us something to live for."

"Well, Vanessa, believe it or not, I was considering selling. A million dollars sounds pretty good right about now."

"What?" She stopped her chopping duty and laid the knife gently onto the counter where she worked. Her back was turned toward the potatoes.

"Well, yeah. After our fight the other day, I made myself a game plan. Part of it was to sell." Vanessa stood tall when I began talking. "Yep, I had it all figured out. I have nothing here anymore. I figured I'd split. Walk away, do the right thing."

"Oh, and you think doing the right thing is this, running away? Like some lame penance for your past sins?"

"Sort of." I backed up against the counter and leaned on it with my butt.

"Well, then what? You were just gonna wash your hands of this diner? Bobby's? Bobby?" She was getting all riled up again and I knew I was no match for Vanessa when she was like this.

"All I'm sayin' is I think everyone would be happier if—"

"Oh, I get it," she interrupted me. "*Now* you're thinking of everyone else's happiness. When she emphasized the word 'now' I knew what she was implying. I just raised my hands with a surrendering motion. But then I didn't need to imply anything after a second when she said, "Well, aren't you the martyr. No, young lady, I don't know what your mother taught you. But mine taught me *you make your bed, you lie in it!* No. You're not selling. I'm not selling. If you're going to atone, you'll do it with me breathing down your neck for the rest of your life. Do you understand me?" She sounded like the momma I'd always dreamed of—hard, but with a soft river running under her skin.

"So, now you're gonna tell me how I'm gonna live out the rest of my life, is that it?"

"Well, at least for today. We have dinner to serve tonight. Get back to work!" She grabbed a tea towel and snapped it at my behind. We would have the diner together for one more night anyway.

Vanessa loved being strong and being in control

and she grew an inch each time she took charge of a situation. This was one way we differed. I admired her. I admired my dead husband's ex-wife.

Chapter 13

José had worked at the diner since he was a young boy. He snuck in over the border as an illegal. But after Vanessa got ahold of him, he got his citizenship papers and a green card, and he worked as a legitimate resident. At the time, his entire family lived in Mexico. He would send money to them monthly to help out. Bobby and I would clean out our closets annually and fill boxes up with clothing we no longer wore. José would ship them down to his mother and father, sisters and brothers, nieces, and nephews.

Bobby and Vanessa took José in when he had no one else to turn to. He'd come up from Phoenix where immigration laws were tightening like a noose around businesses who hired illegals. But a little more north in a small, out-of-the-way town, authorities just seemed to look the other way. José was solid and dependable. He showed up like clockwork. Vanessa taught him better English than what he knew when he got to the states.

Bobby and José always fantasized about a garden in the back of the diner. Bobby even went so far as to buy a few books to learn about vegetable gardens. He and José would draw out plans and dream about the layout, the fresh food, the smells—all the loveliness a vegetable garden brings. But they never got around to it while he and Vanessa were still married. After the divorce, they had to hire an extra person for the kitchen.

So, when Bobby started building our garden, I told him I could help him build the diner's. Well, neither Bobby nor José had one extra second to help, but they did it anyway. I worked early in the morning when the day was cool and they would help out after their shifts, even when the sun was scorching hot. We finished the enclosure one Sunday and Monday, built the potato bin the following Sunday and Monday. After we rototilled the ground and turned the soil with added organics, we began setting stakes and putting in raised gardens and walkways around the garden; we even added bloomers so we could have fresh-cut seasonal flowers on the tables. The overall enclosure had two entrances. One entrance allowed enough room for a person to walk through and the other allowed larger pieces of equipment through, if need be. The larger entrance had a double gate. The smaller, a single gate with a lovely arching arbor where we planted esperanza—a flowering shrub with a name meaning "hope" in Spanish. The esperanza was likely to grow up and over the structure. Hummingbirds couldn't resist its yellow trumpet flowers, but the deer wouldn't touch it—when they came around. Every so often I'd see a doe walking in the distance, but the noise from the highway and the bustle around the building usually kept them away for the most part.

Within a matter of a few weeks we started producing annual flowers and, of course, vegetables. Lettuce sprung up like weeds, so did the broccoli and green onions. Within three months of building our garden, we were using most everything we grew in our restaurant.

People loved it. We loved it. José loved it.

Bobby almost changed the name of the diner to *Jardin de Jose*. I talked him out of it. Thinking back, I might've been wrong. But at the time *Bobby's* seemed the best, even with the new garden. *Bobby's* is what people knew the restaurant to be. Changing the name would change the customer base, I thought. We never told José. I wish we had.

People started to hear about our beautiful garden in the back. José would sneak people outside and around, so Bobby didn't know. He wouldn't have minded, but José worried he might. José would sell tomatoes and lettuce to some of our customers. He'd say, "Mr. Carlisle, someone gives you money for veggies!" He'd shove the cash in Bobby's hand and walk away like a new father, beaming and all.

One day José called very early and woke us. He'd learned his mother had died and had to get to her funeral. We did all we could to assist him in his time of need. That's when we found out José had been selling vegetables on Sundays when we were closed. Every Monday we'd come to work to find a pile of cash in the tip jar. Everyone loved Mondays because the waiters and busboys not only had the regular tips but also the already-filled tip jar at the cashier's counter. No one would ever fess up to it. We didn't put it together until José was out of the picture for a few days.

Arnie, one of our regulars, had heard about José's mother and asked what we were going to do about Sunday.

"Sunday?" Bobby said to Arnie. "We're closed on Sundays."

"So, we don't get our weekly veggies?"

"What are you talking about?"

"Out of the garden, you know, José's been selling vegetables and flowers. It's a real farmer's market, by God! We think it's a great idea, Bobby." Arnie was talking like it was Bobby's idea. Then it all dawned on the three of us, right then and there. Everything fell into place. How we never seemed to have any wasted vegetables, how the money appeared like a coin left under a pillow by the tooth fairy after losing a tooth, how everyone loved to talk to José, how we kept getting new plants even when we didn't remember ordering any. We were so busy with the diner, you see, we weren't worrying about our thriving garden. We weren't missing cash; we were getting it. No inventory was stolen; things seemed off, but fun. Not bad, like we had a dishonest employee or nothing. So, we looked away.

Well, after José got back, the jig was up. When we confronted him, he looked like a beaten puppy. He started taking off his apron like we were firing him.

"That's right, José!" Bobby said it real mean. "You get off your apron off and…" he paused for a second, "put your garden gloves on and get to work! We have a busy Sunday ahead of us in a couple of days and we can't have our little market in shambles!" José's face looked like one big question mark. When Bobby broke into laughter, José realized he was happy about everything. But he kept saying like a forgiven sinner, "Thank you, Mr. Carlisle, thank you."

"Holy Jehoshaphat, José. You're the best. Get out and have fun in your garden. Now go!"

He'd returned the day before from the funeral and Bobby wanted to make sure he had something to live for again. I know how you feel when you lose your mother, like you've lost half your body.

We've kept up José's tradition. Any money he makes from vegetable sales and which aren't reinvested in new plants, we stuff into the tip jar. And I'll bet you any amount, we have the only employees who fight to get a shift in on Mondays.

Chapter 14

He was big, mean looking, and homely as a baboon. He didn't give a name, why would he? He just appeared like an apparition in a horror movie. He had pockmarks from acne past and when he talked, his tight skin pulled in odd directions, not like supple, soft skin, but like he'd been burnt on a spinning wagon wheel. You wanted to feel sorry for the guy, but he had lava in his veins, hot and raging. So, you felt scared instead.

Vanessa seated him back in the corner like he'd requested. He ate a sandwich and drank one beer after the other, for two-and-a-half hours till mostly everyone was gone. That's when he asked to speak with the owner. Vanessa told him she was the owner.

"What can I help you with?"

"This place is sweet." He sucked on a pickle when he said it, like he was sucking someone's dick.

"Thank you, sir, we think so." Vanessa was taken aback a little but remained cool and began to walk away.

"It'd be a shame if anything were to happen to it."

She stopped suddenly and turned back to him. "Excuse me?"

"I don't think I stuttered, ma'am. You think about what I said, now." He slid to the edge of the seat to stand. "How safe are you here running a business like this, being a woman and all. You could get hurt. If I was you, I think I'd sell to the first person who made me an offer." He got up next to her slow and so close she could smell his rancid breath. "You have a good day now." He wiped his mouth with his napkin and threw it onto the seat.

Vanessa stood speechless as he pushed by her out of the restaurant and got in his shiny, black Yukon. Its windows were dark so you couldn't see inside. She walked just outside the doors as he was pulling out of the parking lot. The license plates had been removed from the back.

****

"Georgette?"

"Mm, hmm?" I was cleaning up in the kitchen after the lunch rush and didn't look up.

"We've just been threatened."

"Hmm." I was intent on reordering the kitchen and didn't quite catch what Vanessa had said. "I'm sorry, Vanessa, I didn't catch that. What did you just say?" I stopped wiping and put my hair behind my ears.

"We've been threatened—to sell. He said if we didn't sell, we'd be hurt."

"What?"

"That's right. Some big lug nut just came in, ate lunch, poured about a keg of beer into his mouth, and then threatened us if we didn't sell."

"That's ridiculous."

"I'm telling you, Georgette. It's what just happened."

"Who waited on him?"

"I did."

"Why?"

"He just started ordering after I sat him in the

73

booth, and so I brought it out to him. Easy enough, I thought."

"Did anyone else see him?"

"Oh, I'm sure they all saw him. He looked like he'd been run down by horses pulling a wagon full o' ugly!"

"Vanessa."

"Georgette. This guy was nasty. All pockmarked and everything."

"Vanessa, a person can't help something like that!"

"Inside too. That's not the point. He threatened our business, you and me, get it?"

"It's just so hard to believe. Why would anyone want to threaten us?"

"I don't know. But something's not right." Vanessa left the kitchen.

When I'd finished wiping down the counters, I went out to talk to her again. She was standing at the front door looking out. She had one hand up to her mouth and the other on her hip and looked like she was in another world.

I noticed something I hadn't seen in her before. From how she sat, she looked to be deep in thought and smaller somehow. Before, she'd always looked bigger-than-life to me. I guess because I always felt a little ashamed around her since Bobby, and all. But, for a brief moment, she looked fragile.

"Has he been back?"

I'd startled her from her demons.

"No. Not yet."

"Hey, Van. Let's try not to worry about this, okay? It's a distraction we don't need. Nothing's gonna happen. Don't you give it another thought."

She turned away and clasped both her arms around the front of her like she got a chill down her spine. "Have you counted the till?"

"Huh-uh."

"Well, don't you think it'd be a good idea if you did?

Come on, Vanessa, let's close this place up, okay?"

"Sure. Of course, you're right. What's gotten into me? He really had me going for a second. What time is it?" She looked at her watch. "Oh, Christ! I'm supposed to be at Roberta's tonight. She wants me to help her with some things around the house, you know, some of Rick's things. Sounds fun, doesn't it? Wanna come?" When she saw my face lighten up and actually consider being included, she quickly rescinded the question. "Oh, I'm joking. I'm certain Roberta would prefer to be alone with her mother." She said it like it was a sentence in prison. But for me, being included would have been like water to a parched animal in the desert.

"Oh, I wasn't actually thinking I would go, Vanessa. What's gotten into you?" I turned it around on her. "That guy really got under your skin, didn't he?" She rubbed her arms and went back to the cash register to finish her day, and I went back into the kitchen to take inventory for the next. My gut hurt like someone had punched me. My gut and my heart.

Chapter 15

When Roberta pushed off the floor from packing a box, her face was beet red. Vanessa could see how the divorce had taxed her. She'd lost a lot of weight. Her eyes looked sallow and empty. It seemed she needed a break from reality, needed to leave the house which was once hers and Rick's together. Get away for a while, maybe. Vanessa knelt on the bedroom floor while her daughter lashed out in front of her.

"She feeds on families like a fox in a chicken coop, Mother!" A globule of spit flew from her mouth and she wiped her lips with her arm.

"Roberta, you do have a knack for the dramatic, dear. I think instead of engineering you should've gone into theatre."

"Mother!"

"Roberta, your father and I—"

"Were perfect together!"

"Honey, no marriage is perfect." She looked up at her daughter's angry face and thought how much she looked like Bobby. Vanessa could tell Roberta knew what she insinuated. She turned away from her mother and walked out of the bedroom. The strong footfall lessened as Roberta walked farther down the hall, through the kitchen, and out the back door. From her daughter's bedroom, Vanessa heard the screen door slam and a metal chair scraping along the concrete patio in the back, and then it stopped.

Roberta and Rick had lived in the house for a long time. Vanessa forgot about when and how two people could collect all the mementos filling all the drawers and shelves, crates and hangers, boxes in the garage and attic. But by the end of today, with her help, they would supposedly cut the collection in half. Half Rick's, half Roberta's.

Rick had been commuting for years to a job in Las Vegas. He'd wanted to move there for years, but Roberta would have nothing to do with relocating from the town she'd grown up in, her family, her friends. Also, Rick's position in another town offered her a place to get away with him for extended weekends. Rick's condo in Vegas had a pool and no maintenance, so for Roberta it was like taking a vacation. For Rick, it was still work. Over the past year, Vanessa would listen to her daughter as she cried and complained about repeated arguments and Rick's insistence for her to move there completely. In the end, he got his way but had to leave his wife to get it. He wanted to remain friends with Roberta, and she was completely insulted by the notion. She couldn't believe she would soon have to check the box "divorced" on applications or refer to Rick as her ex-husband. Roberta seemed blindsided by it, but Vanessa saw it coming long ago. Her daughter was self-centered but good-hearted, selfish but loving, intimidating but kind. She would watch Rick when Roberta talked; he seemed ill at ease anymore and quick to anger. He would take off shortly after dinner leaving the women alone to hide out in his office. They hadn't made love much in recent months— he was pulling away—and Roberta was sincerely surprised when a man came to the door to serve her with divorce papers.

Vanessa looked around Roberta's bedroom now. She remembered how difficult her own separation had been on Roberta, and now she was living it all over again. Vanessa had survived her divorce from Bobby, but Roberta never completely forgave her father for leaving. Even now, Vanessa believed Roberta still didn't seem to understand the ways of married people. Roberta definitely was not around during the initial fall of her parents' marriage at eighteen when she went off to college. She was too busy with her and Rick's plan to marry not long after they returned from school. As Vanessa sat on the edge of the bed and looked around, she remembered the sadness upon accepting the fact her marriage to Bobby was about to end. It was imminent, but when Georgette came along, she blamed it on her anyway. Georgette's only fault in the divorce was one of timing. She came too soon.

"Roberta." Vanessa got up slowly as her daughter's name slipped wearily from her mouth. She decided to tell her now before it was too late.

Roberta sat alone and looked hopelessly onto the arid landscape. Only a few yucca and crepe myrtle were left blooming. Every other plant took on its usual olive hue or brown bark. The cactus garden was filled with thick-skinned, prickly succulents of light buttery yellow to dark magenta. Her head was propped up in one hand on the arm of her chair and her feet were flung up onto the glass table. The skin on her ankle above her sock was tan and smooth. A sunbather from long ago, she remembered Roberta had just spent a final weekend with Rick in Vegas ten days before. Vanessa watched her for a second through the door, then walked out as she said, "Roberta, honey, we need to talk."

She looked up at Vanessa and her hand dropped from beneath her chin. "Grab a chair, Mom." Vanessa pulled another chair around, so it was directly facing her daughter. She leaned forward. With both elbows on her legs, she grabbed her hands in front of her.

"Honey, I know this is hard. It was hard for me too. But at least I could see it coming."

"What are you saying?"

"Come on now. You know your dad and I were living out the decline of our marriage when Georgette came along."

"No, Mother, I didn't know that. Are you saying you would have probably gotten a divorce even if Dad hadn't been screwing around on you?"

"Roberta. Please."

"Well, what would you call it, Mother? *Sleeping*?"

"Good Lord, Roberta. You can be so cruel when you want."

Roberta looked away momentarily and then looked back.

"I'm sorry. I just want you to know something. With your father and me there were signs, big signs. I wasn't blind to it. I saw. I saw.

"He didn't want me anymore, you know, sexually. He stayed at the diner until well after it closed doing things I felt could wait or things we could have done together. Then I realized, he didn't want to be around me anymore. I guess I changed after you left. I got a little selfish."

Roberta's eyes gleamed with moisture.

"Anyway, honey, I was getting older and feeling it.

So, I went to the stylist for my nails, for hair coloring, facials, and massages. It wasn't like we didn't have the money. We did. But I wanted to do things to make the aging less, how do I say it, impactful my empty-nester self wasn't handling just the two of, your dad and I well.

Vanessa took in a breath. She was staring at the past and remembering. "I forgot about your father and his needs. He was working a lot and I was playing a lot. By the time you left, we'd gotten a relief cook and I was living it up on my time off. Bobby was tired but he still went in everyday like clockwork. I sort of ignored him. If he couldn't arrange time off, I'd take vacations without him. I'd go alone on cruises, beaches of Mexico, Canada, wherever I wanted. I thought I *deserved* it." She paused again this time shaking her head. "Well, he'd been saying for a while how he was thinking about selling the diner. He'd bring it up and I'd shoot it down. We wouldn't have the income if we sold and I was liking the money. I blew it off and acted like he wasn't serious, but he was. He wanted out as much as I enjoyed *being* out. He was stuck, not me. I didn't realize how serious he was."

"Mother, it still doesn't justify what he did to you."

"That's right, Roberta, what he did to *me*. Not you. Your father and I and our divorce have nothing to do with you. I wish, oh, how I wish, you would get over blaming him for something you really know nothing about."

"My God. I'm in so much pain right now and you're yelling at me?"

"I was in a lot of pain, too, honey. But I didn't have anyone to cry to. So please stop acting like a child and get on with your life. Rick's gone; get over it. Bobby left; I got over it. But you? You hung on as if it were you who was married to him, not me. What happened between your father and me was *our* divorce, not yours. This," Vanessa swept her hands gesturing through the room, "*This* is yours. Start dealing with it like a grown-up, honey. The sooner you come to grips with it, the sooner you'll get over it."

Vanessa stood up in front of her daughter, stepped into her, patted her shoulder, and kissed her on the forehead.

"Call me when you're serious about packing up his things. I'll be over in a flash. Bye, sweetheart."

Vanessa understood Roberta was flummoxed by her mother's forthrightness. She would be angry at first and she'd think about all the comebacks she could say to Vanessa when they saw each other next. She would manifest scenarios she could play out to some imagined finale. But in the end, Roberta would understand why her mother confessed her and Bobby's sordid past. Vanessa knew she would understand. She knew this much about her daughter.

From inside the kitchen window, she watched as Roberta rested her head in her palm, put her feet back up, and did the thing she guessed she'd been doing a lot of these days—she cried.

Chapter 16

Everyone from the gas station to the grocery store was out in front when I arrived at work—everyone, including the police. They were hanging yellow crime scene tape around a couple of the store entrances—the mercantile and the pet store. I was watching while I leaned against my car in the diner's parking lot. For fifteen minutes people milled about with their hands to their mouths. Talking closely together, talking in groups of twos, then threes. Milling, talking, going up to the police, heading back to their group of two or three. Milling. José drove up in his rusted-out sedan. Dirt powdered up and wafted like a ghost off in a breeze when his car rolled from the paved road onto the gravel parking lot. I turned my head away to avoid the dust while still keeping my eye on the fuss going on. He parked next to me in front of the diner. Our sign was bigger than the other signs down the strip—teal blue with red lettering. It never failed to make me laugh when I saw our sign; it looked like it was screaming to passers-by to pull off the road and come in.

"What's happening, Mrs. Carlisle?" Only then, when he said Mrs. Carlisle, it struck me how José must have called Vanessa "Mrs. Carlisle" too.

"I don't know, José."

"The police are there?"

"Yep. I wonder what happened."

"Would you like me to find out, Mrs. Carlisle?"

"Let's find out together." We walked together not speaking for about two hundred yards to where the commotion was. We approached Markus from the gas station first. He didn't see us walk up.

"Hey, Markus."

"Oh, hey, Georgette. Can you believe this?"

"What happened?"

"Vandals. They ransacked a couple stores and set fire to one of the stock rooms."

"Oh, my God." Vanessa was going to flip out.

"They think they might have latent prints so they're going to take them back to the lab and see if they can find a quick match. They got one off the back door, they axed it down." He sounded like a wannabe lawman.

"They axed it?"

"Uh-huh. Wanted in pretty bad, I guess." Markus looked at me sternly. I could hear concern behind his words.

"Did anyone get hurt?"

"No. No, thank the Lord, huh? No one got hurt; it's a blessing, really. A blessing." Markus wandered away muttering about how good it was no one got axed to death in the process. José shadowed me as I worked my way in closer to the action.

Then, Willy, one of the police officers, came out carrying a plastic bag. An orange sticker on it read *EVIDENCE.* He tried to cloak it under his jacket.

"Hey, Willy." I acted like I didn't notice.

"Hello, Mrs. Carlisle." I was expecting him to call me Georgette. He hadn't called me Mrs. Carlisle since Bobby's funeral. I presumed he wanted to show some professionalism.

"Willy, did anyone see the person responsible for this?"

"Person, Georgette? Do you know something you want to tell me?" he asked more hopefully than accusingly.

"No, that's not what I meant. Person, people. Did anyone see anyone?"

"No one's come forth with any information yet. Why do you ask, Georgette? Did you?"

"No." I started chewing on a fingernail. "No, I didn't see anything, Willy."

Willy walked over to one of the police cars, and when he pulled out the baggy I could see it contained two tiny dead animals but I couldn't tell exactly what they were; blood was smeared on the inside and made it difficult to tell for sure. At the same time, I noticed, I heard José gasp.

"Come on, José. We'd better get to work. There's nothing here we can do."

As I turned him away, José whispered, "Oh, Mrs. Carlisle, those poor little animals. Were they dead?"

"Come on, José. Don't look." He kept looking over his shoulder with a look of terror and sorrow all mixed together.

****

Vanessa was a half hour late to work. Roberta was with her, tailing her and saying she was wrong to have done it! By now, I was becoming accustomed to Roberta's outbursts and overreaction to everything. She was nearly forty, my age, but in my estimation, she acted much younger than that. Since the advent of her divorce, she was on high alert. No one was comfortable around her lately and now she was carrying on again.

Vanessa rolled her eyes and walked in front of Roberta, past me into the office. "Mother! This is really not cool!"

"Oh, Christ, Roberta. Give it a rest. It's done, and you have no say in this matter anyway. So, please quit acting out." She huffed out of the office with Roberta tailing her.

"I may not have any say in this, but…but…" She looked around at me and continued, "But Georgette does!" She was nailing her mother by using me. Vanessa's shoulders dropped and she turned slowly back to face her daughter.

"I really hope you're leaving now."

"Well, ask her, Mom. Ask her if she thinks it's a good idea."

Vanessa took a deep breath and turned to me. I was still standing in the doorway between the restaurant and the kitchen. I shrugged my shoulders, raised my eyebrows, and made some helpless motion with my hands, not understanding the problem. Vanessa walked up to me square in the face.

"I bought a gun. You mind?"

We were standing face-to-face, but the showdown was between Van and her daughter. She looked weakened by the confrontation and I knew she needed a cohort in this so-called crime.

"Oh, good. You got it?" So, I lied.

I winked at her so Roberta wouldn't see. Vanessa smiled smugly, turned to look at Roberta, and opened her hands as if to gesture *see*? Then all hell broke loose.

"You're okay with this?" Roberta rushed up to both of us but directed her ire at me.

"Your mother and I both make decisions around here, Roberta, you know that. A gun will give us a little added protection. What with all the burglaries and whatnot, it seems like a fine idea."

I looked back at Vanessa, "Just like we discussed, right, Van?" Her mother was beaming like she'd witnessed the second coming or something.

"You two don't fool me. I know you didn't know anything about it; you're just lying for her. What a brown-noser!" The pendulum had swung the other way and now the wrath was upon me.

Van said, "Roberta, watch your mouth. Please, darling!"

Roberta stormed out.

After we heard the front door slam shut, I turned to Vanessa.

"You bought a freaking gun? What the hell has gotten into you?"

The mood broke and Vanessa was flailing her arms and *this'n and that'n* and all. I shook my head when she was finished because I knew she wasn't about to take the thing back and get a refund. She was scared. She reacted because she was scared.

"Let me see it." As we walked toward the office, she sounded like a kid in a candy shop.

"It's sweet, Georgie, it's pretty, too, pretty and powerful, a .357 magnum. Shiny as a new bike."

And she was right. It was pretty. Pretty dangerous. I was fretting just to have it near me.

"Do you know how to use it?"

"I used to go shooting with my father. He'd take my brother and me to a place not too far from here, Ben Avery's Shooting Range. If I recall correctly, I wasn't so bad." Hearing she had a brother again made me realize how little I knew about Vanessa. Was he still alive? Was he dead?

"Well, I've never even seen a real gun, let alone shot one."

"Then we'll have to get you some lessons. It wouldn't hurt me any to take a refresher course either. We can go out and shoot it together. It'll be fun. Really."

I couldn't believe how giddy she was acting about this stupid gun. Guns had always been taboo with my momma. She'd seen a man shot down in the streets of Milledgeville and she reminded me every time the subject of guns came up, whether on TV or in politics. So, I was always a little afraid of them, respectful, if you will.

"You're a woman among women, Van, I'll hand you that."

Chapter 17

The diner's garden had grown into a jungle of colors, smells, and tastes. Plants were growing at nuclear rates. We had knobby squash, beefsteak tomatoes, curly leaf lettuce. Just about anything we needed or wanted on a dish, we had growing in back of the diner. José had come straight from Manzanillo, Mexico, way down in south Mexico, where he was a gardener at some chi-chi resort for tourists. He had a green thumb the size of a melon and when he wasn't bussing tables inside, you could find him outside weeding, turning soil, pulling ripened edibles, and talking to his *bambinos* as he called them. José would sing Mexican folk tunes while he worked the garden. He said, *"Hace que crecen grandes y fuertes!"* Which meant "makes his babies grow big and strong."

Over the years, José taught me lots of Spanish. In fact, after working with him for a couple years, when we'd see each other we'd go right into the conversation of the language. I will always have José to thank for helping me learn another country's native tongue and expanding my mind, not to mention, my horizons.

José never missed a day of work except when his momma died. Aside from that, he never missed a single day, never came in late, and didn't ever call in sick. He loved working here in the garden.

Then came one of the saddest days ever. I didn't

make the connection at the time. It had been about a week after the man from Chariot came offering to buy our little business, our booming little business, the one worth two point five million dollars.

****

"Mrs. Carlisle!" José's voice sounded frantic over the telephone line.

"Yes, José. What is it?"

"Oh, Mrs. Carlisle. Something terrible, just terrible."

As quick as a thumb snap José reverted to his native tongue.

"Slow down, José. Tell me what happened. In English."

"I came to work and found the most awful thing."

"What is it, José?"

"The garden, Mrs. Carlisle, the garden has been destroyed."

"What?"

"It's true, Mrs. Carlisle. Someone has destroyed our precious little garden." He sounded like he would cry if I didn't say something quickly.

"Okay, José. Don't worry. I'll be right there. I'm still in bed. So, give me a couple of minutes. Okay?"

"Yes, Mrs. Carlisle. I'll be here waiting for you."

For a moment, I sat back in bed not believing what I'd just heard. Gangster moved off my chest and nuzzled deep into the pillow next to me. The phone call had disturbed his morning slumber. The clock's red digital display told me I had two more hours before it became critical to get out of bed. I decided I should call Vanessa, too. She wasn't going to like hearing my voice this early in the morning.

****

Vanessa was already there by the time I got to the diner. It had only taken me twenty minutes to get out of bed, make some instant coffee, wash my face, brush my teeth, and feed the cat. She was standing outside the diner waiting for me. My car skidded when I pressed hard onto the brakes. I jumped out.

"How bad is it?"

"Bad. Come on." We walked quickly behind the restaurant toward the garden.

My heart fell. It looked like someone had driven a truck over a portion of the picket fence enclosure and then did spinouts on top of the plants. Tire treads crossed and crisscrossed the entire spot running east to west, then north to south. José didn't utter a word. He'd been crying and his eyes looked red and swollen. There were streaks down his cheeks where his tears had dried. Vanessa walked around inside picking up bits of fencing material. She walked over to the now leaning garden shed. As she walked up to it, I could see one of the corners of the building had been demolished and looked like someone had taken a huge bite out of it. She disappeared inside for a second, resurfaced with a rake, and began cleaning the mess. José followed suit, disappearing momentarily then reappearing with a wheelbarrow. I was frozen. Still taking in the sacking the garden had endured, I couldn't believe it. Why? The question kept repeating in my head. Why?

"You gonna help or what?" Vanessa had a no-nonsense way about her.

"You think we should call the police?"

"Do you think they'll help us clean this up and get the diner ready in time to open for lunch?"

"I mean, maybe they can help us get whoever did this."

"Georgette, we have less than five hours to get this mess cleaned up and prep for lunch. I'll have to go back home to shower and change."

"I don't need to take a shower."

"Oh, nice. We'll have all sorts of wonderful smells emanating from the kitchen."

José chuckled at Vanessa's snide implication. It was the first time he'd uttered a sound since we'd been there. Walking over the wreckage of our garden reminded me of one of those newsreels on TV when reporters walk through rubble explaining the destruction of a sacred land. I retrieved a black landscape bag from the shed and began sifting through debris, collecting. In the farthest sunniest corner was another potato bin Bobby had made for the restaurant, for me. He'd taken special pride in building the one at the diner. The one at our home was a trial run, but he'd perfected the one for the diner. It was split apart with adolescent potatoes bleeding in between broken slats of wood, spilling out with earth and peat. My legs felt weak and finally I could stand no more. My knees hit the ground first, then my hands. I heard Vanessa say something soft to hold José back. They just let me alone until I was done crying.

Chapter 18

After twenty minutes of washing dirt from around my face, neck, wrists, and ankles, and redressing in a second chef's uniform we kept on hand, my nails still needed a good scrubbing. I realized the only way to make my hands appear clean was to trim off my scrappy-looking nails.

Both José and Vanessa had gone home to get cleaned up, and I'd just barely finished organizing myself and the kitchen when the first customer strolled in. By then José had returned but still no sign of Vanessa, and now I started envisioning something terrible happening to her too. Sandy, one of the waiters, came in and voiced her concerns as well, just not as eloquently as say, I would have.

"The other missus is late!" She sniggered gruffly at her poor taste and picked up her drink order before I could have a go at her, and she must have barely passed by her when Vanessa walked in.

"Sorry I'm late. I went over to the gun shop and got some bullets. I think tonight would be a great night to start your lessons."

"Whatever. Get out there! We have customers already."

Vanessa scrambled to pin her nametag on her blouse and smoothed back her hair. She looked at me, cocked her head, raised her eyebrows, and went to work.

****

"Shooters begin." The firing monitor called out the instruction over the loudspeaker. Vanessa picked up the gun and reassembled it, loaded it, and handed it to me. Within seconds, gunfire cracked and exploded all around us. Single steady shots. Quick and repeating shots. I jumped. It seemed second nature to her the way she managed it. But I pressed my arms firmly by my side.

"Take it! Just listen to me. I'll talk you through it. Stand like I showed you." She shoved the gun toward me, and I took it reluctantly. She glared at me to begin. "Now hold it gently like an egg, okay?" She handed the gun over to me and my heart started to pound like a bongo, my hands were shaking and sweaty.

"I don't know about this, Van." I turned to the target out in the field, and with my right foot in front of my left, and my arms steady out but not locked stiff, I took the stance.

"Good. Good. Now, loosen your grip. You're not trying to strangle it."

I looked at her with squinted eyes and when I did, the gun went off. I screamed. It nearly blew me off my feet. A carbon and smoke smell filled the air and some of the gunpowder kicked out into my face and eyes. They began to water instantly.

"Holy crap!" I rubbed my eyes with my shoulders, the right one first, then the left.

"Pay attention to what you're doing! This isn't a Barbie doll." Panic coursed over me in a hot wave. I looked at Vanessa with wide eyes.

"You have mascara all over your face." She smiled

because I think she could tell I was about ready to cry. "Be serious and keep focused on the gun, not me." Her words softened. "Don't feel intimidated. I'm trying to teach you, not intimidate you, okay? You're holding a weapon, Georgie. Always, but always, keep this one fact in mind. Let me show you." She took the gun from me, stood firm, twisted her head to line up with the sight, closed her non-aiming eye, and squeezed the trigger, BAM! She squeezed again. BAM! "See? Like that. Now you try."

"I don't want to."

"Quit your sniveling and take it." She said it like a drill sergeant, and I responded like a Private First Class.

"Okay, now, once again, take your stance. That's right. Hold it up. Higher, Georgie, you're aiming at the ground. That's better. Can you see the sight? Is it lined up with the target? Okay, now slowly and controlled, squeeze the trigger." The moment of firing was one of the most frightening yet exhilarating feelings I've ever experienced. I hit the target.

"I did it!"

"Why, yes you did. I'll be damned. Okay, you have two more rounds. Now, empty that sonofa...But before she could say it, I took the stance, aimed fast, and pulled the trigger. BAM. Then again. BAM. I looked to see if I'd hit the target. Only one more hole from me. I missed either the first or the second shot. I wasn't sure.

"You hit the second one perfectly." Vanessa was an old pro at this I could tell.

"That spray feels really weird."

"The gunpowder? Yeah. You get used to it though. Let's reload and shoot some more, what d' ya say?"

"Okay."

****

The first black stout went down like cream. Vanessa's lesson started off a little shaky but after alternating ten rounds with her, I'd come to understand how powerful these things actually were. It reminded me of the quote, "Guns don't kill people, people do." But I still had a sneaking suspicion the guns had something to do with it.

Vanessa had followed me home. I told her the least I could do for her after two proper southern ladies spent a day out on the shooting range was to buy her a nice cold beer. She stayed for a little more than an hour and we had two beers. We talked a little about business but mostly about the gun, about shooting the gun, and about how invigorated it made us both feel—the blood pulsing through our veins and all! We sat and talked, drank beer, and talked, talked about nothing in particular. She told me about her brother. He'd moved to Washington and had a thriving little business close to the base of Mount St. Helens. He was killed because he refused to leave his home after warnings the once dormant volcano was going to blow. He had two acres of wooded land only a mile from his business. The volcano erupted one mid-May day in 1980 and sprayed magma over two thousand feet in the air. When the stuff came back down to Earth, his home was buried under hot rock and mud from the blast. Although they couldn't find a body—everything buried got baked beyond recognition—they assumed he perished.

She didn't add much but I knew more about Vanessa, more than she revealed. I remembered the letter she'd written to Bobby was dated shortly after her brother was killed. Even now, when she talked of him, the memory bubbled to the surface. She got misty but acted as though she had gotten a lash or something in her eye. I'd never seen Vanessa get emotional, not until the day we went shooting together.

Chapter 19

Early evening was hanging with white flies
clustered like clouds in the warm air. When they
landed, they'd do so on innocent hibiscus and lantana.
At the cabana bar, Tweeter took a long drink from his
Long Island iced tea. He liked to meet clients at
Houston's. The place was classy and stood in stark
contrast to his unsophisticated manner. People gave
Tweeter room when he'd walk in and when he'd sit at
the bar, which was fine with him. Having space meant
having fewer eavesdroppers. Pinzer walked in and
spotted him right away on the business side of the bar
near the waitress pickup station by the straws, olives,
lemon peels, and lime wedges. Tweeter tipped his head
up in recognition of Pinzer. Tweeter couldn't help but
feel envious of Pinzer's appearance, clean-cut, carrying
an attaché, the appearance Tweeter thought exemplified
money.

As Pinzer approached, he consciously had to fix his
facial expression not to intimate to him how Tweeter's
appearance nauseated him.

"Hey, man. How's it goin'?" Pinzer sounded cool
about the meeting, which immediately set Tweeter at
ease, and he put his hand out to shake.

"Good. Can I buy you a drink?"

Pinzer nodded. "Sure."

"What'll it be?"

"You having the usual?"

"Uh-huh. Long Island iced tea."

"I think I'll just have a German pilsner."

"I'll have another," Tweeter yelled off to the bartender.

"So, how'd it go?" Pinzer wanted to get done with this meeting as quickly as possible.

"Easy. Went off without a glitch. Did you hear anything?" The bartender delivered both the men's drinks.

"Pyle said the police think it's some teenage vandals. They haven't got a clue. Both women are shaken up by it. It's time to go back and make a second offer." Pinzer grabbed his beer like an Oscar, held it up in a toast and took a long healthy drink.

"You have the money?" Tweeter looked at Pinzer and his bright, scarred face distorted in in a macabre way. Pinzer looked away.

"Yeah, yeah. Here." He reached into his briefcase and pulled out an envelope. "Don't count it here. It's all there, ten thousand, like we agreed."

Tweeter stood and pulled a wad of cash from his pocket, counted out twenty dollars in fives and threw it onto the bar. "Perfect." Tweeter sucked down his drink while he stood. "Call if you need anything else."

As Tweeter began to walk away, Pinzer nodded he would and picked up his beer to take another swallow. "Will do."

He turned to see Tweeter leave and felt a shiver run down his spine, like a rattler had just crawled out of his pants.

Chapter 20

As he packed, the mayor's head sweated profusely from his rapid and exaggerated pace and he wiped it off with the sleeves of his upper arms. He balled two dress shirts one after the other and stuffed them into his pullman tote. Helen leaned against the bedroom door biting her thumbnail. He went to another drawer and pulled out his dollar sign boxer shorts and another striped pair, grabbed two pair of black knee socks, and two undershirts. He piled them next to his piece of luggage before stuffing them in along and down the inner sides of the two-day hodgepodge of things to wear. He grumbled and shook his head angrily while he packed.

Finally, he stopped and looked at Helen again and protested further.

"What were you thinking, if anything, by going out on 'a night with the girls,' as you put it?"

Helen's hand lowered from her mouth as if she wanted to defend herself, but no words were readily available. She shrugged her shoulders, hemmed, and hawed, but only for want of an excuse the mayor would approve of. Helen knew an excuse didn't exist, and she looked out through the door where she stood. She slowly brought her thumbnail back in between her teeth and chewed on it more.

"Are you stupid or something?"

Helen turned quickly toward him from the cruelty and squinted disapproval.

"Well, really, Helen, did you think it was a good idea to go out drinking with them?

"Why not, Harold?"

"Why not! I'll tell you why not—you're supposed to be the wife of an esteemed politician." She turned her head away and rolled her eyes so he couldn't see. "And here you are, carrying on like common folk, that's why not!"

He was again stepping up onto the soapbox, which happened more often than not during their life together since his career move into the political arena, a move she'd long regretted.

Then, Helen began meagerly, "I'll tell you one thing, Harold, going out with them, as you put it, was one of the most fun times I've had in...I can't remember. I don't know when it was I laughed so hard. We had fun, Harold. Fun, plain, and simple." Helen got a touch bolder. "I'm sorry if this upsets you, but I'm not sorry I did it."

"You certainly have changed from the woman I married. I remember when you wanted nothing more than to please me, be my wife, and support my efforts, efforts I make for us. But I see these women are more important to you than I am."

"Oh, Harold, for crying out loud. Can you get more theatrical?" She spoke out daringly.

"Excuse me, Mrs. Pyle!"

"Quit yelling at me, Harold. It's demeaning."

"I'm demeaning you? You demeaned me when you went out on your drinking binge!"

"Harold, please, it wasn't a binge. We had a couple

of glasses of wine at their restaurant. No one was around except the three of us. We made dinner there together and had a good time just being women."

"Just women, Helen. Well, let me remind you, my dear, you are not just any woman. You, Helen, are the wife of the mayor in this here town and you'd better start behaving like it again."

Threatening was always a last resort with Harold in any confrontational scenario, but mostly with Helen, and she hated it. She walked out when he finished.

As she sat at the kitchen table, her tea wafted up in steamy spikes and smelled of bergamot. Her journal's pages were rice-paper thin from rigorous writing.

May 3rd: Harold reminds me of a Tyrannosaurus rex: he's a virulent meat-eater and vicious when he wants. He has beady, small eyes and a big open mouth always spouting, roaring, growling ideas of a perfect future, his perfect future. I don't know him anymore. He's become an oddity to me, more interesting than interested. You're my only source of comfort. Your skin touches my hands, and I touch your skin—soft, dry, delicate page who knows me completely. Flannery would never have put up with someone so weak. She would shun a weaker person for a strong writer. Weakness breeds parasites. Parasites eat the body from the inside out. They eat the soul. Your skin—translucent, watermarked linen crisp—my hand caresses you tenderly, tenderly with my sad words.

Forgive me, Flannery. I'm not worthy.

Helen sipped her black and creamed tea and let its fragrance soothe her soul. She closed her eyes before setting the bone china cup back on its saucer. When she reopened her watery eyes, she gazed at her own front yard through the boxwood-lined walkway, the solar lights, the Saltillo stepping-stones. She gazed past the asphalt's pulsing heat of the blackened, pebbly pavement, to the neighbor's triple-tiered wax leaf topiary. Her eyes landed and then skipped off the leaded, cut glass windows, trellised over their seldom-fired chimney into the tips of tall oak and birch beyond a straggled and parched riverbed, out toward the distant sun breaking through the leaves in the trees and splitting off into a crystal blue firmament, away, away, away. The distant land welcomed her, called to her. She could hear the ocean's breeze, waves cresting, ebbing, arcing, flowing, salt air, fish-laden yet clean, mournful gulls crying, boats lolling along, massaged in between green waves slipping out to sea, away, away, away.

She closed her eyes again and held her face in her hands. Why did it seem so utterly impossible?

****

Pyle was in the bathroom collecting the toiletries he'd need for the next couple of days. Before he opened the medicine cabinet, he caught a glimpse of himself in the mirror. The mayor. He was upset with Helen but not as much as with the other women, "the Carlisle wives." He chuckled to himself when he thought it. *Those bitches had better sell. They don't know what they're asking for if they don't.* Women! They should be seen and not heard. They have their place. The only reason they had the diner at all was because of the hard work Bobby had put into it. But they benefit. *It's not right, not right.* He was throwing miniatures of aftershave and shampoo, toothpaste, shaving cream, and deodorant, plus his razor and comb into his leather satchel. That should do it.

****

He walked into the kitchen and broke into her fantasy. "I don't understand you sometimes, Helen. You seem to be regressing rather than maturing. Have you been to the doctor lately? Maybe you should consider seeing someone, someone in Phoenix or Las Vegas. Have you thought of that? Maybe you need therapy or something. You've been off, and I won't stand another bout of Helen's needing this and Helen's needing that. I thought we fixed this issue years ago. When I get back from Phoenix, you'd better have some answers about your behavior and what steps you're going to take in the realm of self-improvement. I'll stop at Border's while I'm there and pick up some self-help books too.

"Well, dear, I have to head out. My appointment is just after lunch and I'm cutting it close as it is. You'll look into some doctors, won't you, Helen? Call someone today and make an appointment, but again make sure he's in Phoenix or Vegas. We mustn't have a scandal, dear. Please try to think less of yourself; you're so selfish anymore. Must go. Goodbye, honey. Kiss, kiss."

He smooched at her. An annoying little habit he had picked up during campaigning so he didn't really have to kiss babies, just the backs of hands if his lips had to touch anything at all. He did the Nixon wave after kissing to crowds with his hand; an almost Hitleresque salute with a little twirl at the end.

Helen looked away when he closed the doors, past the yard, the neighbors, the trees again. She wrote in her journal again with the next line.

Away, away, away.

Susan Wingate

Chapter 21

Gangster was sitting in front of the television set again, watching for screen birds or screen mice or whatever he watched the television screen for. The kitchen was a mess from another day racing from one place to the other, if not the diner, to the grocery store or the post office for stamps. One of those days when you seemed to be behind your behind instead of in front it. After cleaning, I decided to relax for a second. A steaming white teacup filled the air with a sweet vanilla scent and waited for me on the cocktail table next to Gangster.

After wiping down the counter and putting away a few previously used items—a butter knife, a bag of bread, a jar of peanut butter, a plate, and a used napkin—I went to the sofa and patted the couch for the cat to join me.

"Gangster, come here, pal. Sit next to me." He simply ignored me the way cats will.

"Kitty, kitty, kitty." His tail flicked with annoyance and his ears turned back. He refused to be disturbed from his television show.

"Gangster, come on, kitty, come here." I was begging now. He turned slowly and rubbed against the leg of the table and slowly around it to the sofa by me. I leaned to scratch his head all the way down to the tip of his tail and he circled toward me to repeat the consideration. I did.

The TV was rambling away when the doorbell rang. Just before getting up to answer it, a commercial about Phoenix local news came on previewing a spotlight on juvenile crime, and whose face was there on the screen but our own mayor, Harold Pyle. The thought of Pyle being on TV made me giggle as I went to the door. Looking through the peephole, I could see the frail figure of Helen outside.

"Helen? Hi. You won't believe it!" With the door open, I motioned her to join me inside.

"What?"

"I just saw your husband on TV." Helen looked honestly surprised.

"You did? When?"

"Just now. It was a commercial for the news coming up. Why don't you stay and we can watch together?"

"Well, I don't want to impose, Georgette." Gangster welcomed Helen by pushing against her legs once, then twice.

"Hi, kitty."

"That's Gangster, he's the welcoming committee."

"Hello, Gangster." She bent down and caressed his long hair, and he made this breathy cat sound that had a distinct word wrapped in it, like *wow*. She smiled at me when he did.

"I know Gangster was really hoping to watch me sit and read tonight, but I guess we can put up with the imposition! Of course, you're not imposing! I'm happy you popped by. Come in. Would you like to share a pot of tea with me?"

"Sure, sounds nice. I brought this too." She reached

into that big bag of hers and pulled out a frosty bottle of white wine. "I didn't want to bust in on you empty-handed. I think you like chardonnay, right?"

"That's Vanessa's favorite, but I like it too. Oh, fun! How thoughtful. Let's have that! Would you like a glass of wine?" I headed back into the kitchen to get a couple of glasses.

"Sure." Then she transitioned abruptly into a previous topic. "What station?"

"Hmm?"

"What station did you see Harold on?"

"Oh! Sorry, um, five, I think. Channel five. Sit down, they may show it again. I'll be there in a sec." It had been so long since someone had just dropped in on me and I wanted it to at least appear like I knew how to entertain. The deep primary colors of the Chanticleer hand tray were set off against the thick, light wood of the cocktail table. French style napkins and crystal stemmed gold wine glasses added an elegant touch to my southwestern environment. Helen smiled when I presented the wine bucket filled with ice and the bottle of wine set inside it wrapped in a bright yellow tea towel. Returning from my second trip to the kitchen I brought back a triangle of triple cream cheese, some gourmet crackers, and a bowl of grapes.

"There. Have you seen him?"

"Not yet. They'll probably repeat the promo again in a while. Oh, cheers! Thanks, Georgette; this looks lovely."

"Cheers."

Gangster begged between us and I poked at the creamy cheese and let him lick it off my finger.

"He's beautiful."

"He's very spoiled. He can do whatever he pleases around here, for sure."

"This is why we have pets—to have constant and unconditional love and to spoil them for?"

"I suppose so. Oh! There he is, see?" I pointed my attention to the television set.

"Harold." She said it quietly like he'd committed a venial sin.

We watched and waited for the reporter to do her lead-in:

"More and more youths are committing heinous crimes. Normally, we tend to think of this as an urban problem, but urban sprawl is not only a geographical condition, it's a social condition, as well. Mayor Pyle, how do you feel about this issue?

"Well, Linda, our town of Sunnydale may not be big, but we've seen big city issues seeping into the skin of our little community. Sad, really. We've recently been the victim of a series of juvenile offenses. After a string of crimes, we've collected plenty of evidence that tells us we need proactive measures to curb the problem. I'm here today, in Phoenix, to discuss these matters with a few of the good people here. Maybe if we put our heads together, we can come up with a viable solution to this sad situation."

"Thank you, Mayor Pyle."

She turned back to the camera. *"Harold Pyle is the mayor of Sunnydale, Arizona, located about sixty-five miles north of Phoenix.*

Richard, back to you."

"I thought they'd ruled out the kids. Huh." Helen's chin lifted as if offering judgment on his comment. "He never mentioned anything about a TV interview. Harold never ceases to amaze me." She said it almost as if she'd forgotten I was in the room, or if she was in my house. Then, she snapped out of it and looked down to gather her thoughts. "Well," she said as she grabbed her glass and turned my way, "Here's to Harold, politician extraordinaire." Her face showed no emotion, years of practicing in front of the mirror, maybe. Or could it have been she was sad? There was no reading her.

"We really never know anyone, do we, Helen?"

"Boy, that's a fact."

"You know, although Bobby and I were close, there were times he'd seem to vanish from sight, poof! Gone, like that." Snapping my fingers, I continued. "And toward the end, I didn't even know he was sick. He never mentioned any problems with his heart. He kept it from me, a secret."

"We have lots of secrets, some we even try to keep from ourselves." The way she said it made me feel like someone had run me through with a hot poker. She took a slow sip of wine. After she blotted her lips and dug into her tote to find a tube of lip balm, she applied it, then threw it back inside the bag, and placed her big purse down again by the leg of the table. When she did, it remained open like a gaping mouth. Inside I saw a big round bottle of French perfume. There was a pair of soft, brown suede gloves and a journal propped against the side of her purse with a pen attached to its cover. An envelope was slipped tightly under the pen. It had a name written on it; one I'd never heard mentioned before. *Wellen* was written on the envelope in familiar handwriting, but I couldn't place whose. Right then she must have noticed me staring into her bag because she pushed it closed with the side of her leg.

"I write daily."

"God, Helen, I'm so sorry. I shouldn't have been peering inside your purse."

"No, it's okay, really. Not too many people know I write. I've only told one other person."

"Fiction?" Feeling guilty about what had just happened I jumped at her offer to change the subject, a secret subject at that.

"Oh, no, nothing like that. Fiction just seems too difficult, too creative. I don't know. I write in my journal every day and write a few essays when the mood hits me."

"Essays about what?"

"Well, the last essay commented on society's view of beauty. I call it *"Hands of Time."* It begins with a writer looking at her aging hands as she types."

"I'd love to read it someday."

"Really?"

"Oh, yes. I'm an avid reader. Bobby and I used to read to each other. It was very romantic I thought."

"Very intimate. Yes. Sounds lovely."

"May I?"

"What?"

"Read your essay one day."

"Oh, it's very personal. I'm not very good at all, it's just a hobby I have."

"I bet you're very good. What does Harold think of it?"

"Harold! He's never read anything of mine. He'd call me foolish, and I just don't think I could ever let him see anything I've written."

"Helen. I'm sure he'd love your work."

"You don't know Harold."

"Please. He's your husband. He loves you. He'd love whatever you did."

"That's a sweet thought; however, I'm afraid we're not like that. Most everything we do centers around Harold's career, politics. We eat, breathe, and sleep politics."

"Well, when you talk about your day, don't you tell him what you've written?"

"Ha, ha. No. No, I don't." She took another slow drink. I could see how very forlorn she was. "Georgette, you're a very kind woman. I do enjoy your company."

"Yeah, I think we get along just fine, Helen. Here's to new friends, eh?" We clinked our glasses together and sipped to our toast.

"I know now why Bob was so entranced by you. You're quite beautiful and you're so very kind. You have a good heart, Georgette. He used to talk about you all the time."

"Bobby did? You knew him?" I felt the earth shift.

She blushed. "Well, yes, he'd been in town forever! I knew him well, I guess. Actually, I feel like Bob was my only true friend. I knew Vanessa, too. But Bob would sit with me after the restaurant closed and we'd talk. He was a good man. He was kind, like you."

Helen was revealing a past I couldn't quite piece the puzzle to. I felt off-balance. Like the ground was crumbling beneath my feet.

"Why, he never mentioned he knew you. I don't know if it might have ever come up, but you'd think..."

"He mentioned you! Lots. I'm here to tell you, Georgie, after Vanessa, you were all there was for him, ever." Her speech was loosening up and I realized the wine was hitting her.

"So, what did he say about me?"

"Everything! Good lord, you were all he had on his mind. *Georgie this* and *Georgie that*. Hmm…" A little more wine and down to the bottom of her glass.

"Here, have some more." I picked up the bottle by the towel like a sommelier in a restaurant and poured.

"See! That's what I mean. He'd mention stuff like that. He'd say, 'She has the cutest little twang in her voice but it's like she's been all over the world!' And he'd smile and stop talking. It made me crazy. You know, jealous almost. Not because I wanted Bob. Oh no," she laughed. "Nothing anything like that." Her face flushed and she went on, "but because I wanted *that* kind of love, you know? What you two had."

"I think I do."

We'd been talking for nearly an hour when we emptied the bottle. Helen wasn't a woman who could hold her liquor. She was small and probably didn't do too much drinking around Harold. The new friendship we were making was built, in part, by the telling of small secrets through the consumption of fermented grapes. I had the feeling Helen knew more than her fair share of confidences and she parceled them out slowly and suggestively. She simmered, was hot and swampy. You'd never know it until you spent some time with her. But this plain, throwback type woman had an edge.

Chapter 22

"What were you thinking?"

"You said they'd need motivation."

"Yes, but I didn't mean to destroy their property!"

"Don't raise your voice with me, Mayor. You're in this as deep as I am." Zach Pinzer stared right through Harold Pyle. He knew he had tied a Gordian knot in the noose and it was tightening around the mayor's neck.

"I want out. This isn't good."

"You want out. You can't get out. Money's been exchanged, I have contracts signed. We're going through with this, understand? This project will happen, with or without you."

"Without me." He yanked his briefcase from the chair and stormed out, leaving the door wide open.

"Leyla."

"Yes, Zach." She flung her long, blond hair from the sides of her face and tugged at her hemline.

"Sweetheart, get me Tweeter on the phone, will ya?"

"Yes, Zach." She smiled seductively and turned her back to him. "Zach?"

"Yeah." He looked up and she stared back at him. Looking behind her, he loosened his tie.

"Will you come by tonight? I have something you need to see."

"What time?"

"Whenever you get off. Why don't you call? I'll have a nice, hot bath ready for you with a bottle of Moet. I really need you tonight, Zach."

"You better leave early then, sugar. 'Cause I can't wait." He grabbed at his crotch and she sizzled enjoyment before she left his office. "Call Tweeter!" He leaned forward in his seat and yelled to her before the door shut.

****

Harold had been under pressure for months and was still reeling about the conversation with Pinzer when he pulled onto the freeway on-ramp heading out of Phoenix. He made a good impression with the people at Channel Five and no longer had to worry about the likes of Zach Pinzer and his associates. He'd stated publicly his intentions, good intentions. He wanted the women out, sure, but not the way Pinzer meant. He never considered when he suggested Pinzer to handle it, the guy would hire some ape to do his dirty work.

Traffic was treacherous and he slowed before sidling into the flow of merging cars. His mind raced around an excuse, or better yet, an alibi regarding his involvement with Chariot International Incorporated.

"Christ!" He yelled in part because of the speeding sedans, minis, trucks, semis, convertibles, and SUVs, but also in part because he was angry with himself about getting involved with thugs. What was he thinking! How could he have let things get so out of control? His indicator blinked on and off, alerting other drivers of his intention to merge into the middle lane. Back-to-back traffic destroyed his composure. No one cared anymore about anyone else on the road. He barely squeezed in between a large, black vehicle and a red, white, and blue postal van. He hated city driving especially by means of the freeway.

When he returned to Sunnydale, he'd have to lay out a believable defense of his involvement—muddle the money trail, cover his tracks. Pinzer was a loose cannon and couldn't be trusted.

"Bastard!" He flipped off the driver in the black car. Then the car shimmied up close next to Pyle's driver side but traffic slowed him to a safe distance behind him.

Harold listened to himself, sometimes speaking aloud about the wasted paper used to produce different documents to coordinate this deal, getting the letter of intent signed, the earnest money paid, a quit claim deed issued, plat recordings pulled, the closing agreement and escrow instructions filed. Destroying or better yet losing these documents would prove a tricky proposition, but it could be done. He wondered if a 1098, or was it a 1099, had been issued yet. He'd have to check with the accounting department.

The mayor's mind swirled around the complexity of a sale such as this one.

The traffic was relentless. He saw through his rear view the same truck from a few minutes earlier. The driver once again eased into a position closing in on his left. Harold put his elbow on the rim of the window and covered the side of his face with his hand. He promised he would just ignore the previous incident. Harold decided he would slow up so the driver would end up passing him by virtue of the others driving at a steady, fast pace in the next lane.

With his hand hiding his face, the mayor lost himself again in a whirlpool paper trail of contracts, checks, and settlement agreements. But his mind was diverted when he heard a repetitive, insistent honking. The mayor dropped his arm and looked toward the driver making all the noise. The driver of the SUV continued honking. The mayor lifted his hand and shrugged his shoulders in a question mark gesture. The driver honked steadily every so often, looking over and smiling through the dark windows of his car. Harold could see his teeth so he must be smiling.

Harold felt badly about flipping the man off. Then he thought the driver was trying to communicate something to Harold. Maybe something was wrong with his car. Maybe a seat belt was hanging out, a wheel was shimmying, or a taillight was out of commission. Harold could barely see the man's face through the window. The glass was too dark, but he was sure he saw him smile. Then all at once, the SUV took an impetuous swerve toward his car. The mayor reacted fast by jerking the steering wheel nervously to the right almost crossing into a lane with back-to-back traffic. Harold looked angrily over at the black SUV. What the hell was wrong with this guy? The SUV's window rolled slowly halfway down to reveal a large, dark-haired man with black sunglasses. Even from a distance he could see the man's mottled skin. The man motioned for Pyle to lower his window.

Stopping himself from another too-quick-to-act decision, Harold decided to take a couple of deep breaths. He would apologize to this volatile creature, then be on his way.

Harold pressed on the window control, his eyes darting in between the cars in front of him and to the man beside him. But before he could get out his apology, the guy yelled out something to him but Harold couldn't make out his words. From the rush of the cars, the wind took the breath of the driver's voice away, along with the speeding cars.

"What?" the mayor yelled louder. He directed his eyes between the cars in front and the mirror behind, to the passenger side view, and back to the driver of the SUV. Each time the mayor could glance at the man, he was looking at the traffic as well. Finally, the man and he looked at each other, catching their timing just right. The man smiled strangely and shouted something again and again his words were inaudible. "You're...man." But again, the rushing wind swept his words away.

"I'm sorry! I apologize." Harold yelled as loud as his voice could manage. There. That should do help abate the situation. The mayor began rolling up his window, but the man began his incessant honking again.

Then he yelled louder, and the mayor barely could understand the man's entire statement. It was drummed out by more honking, tires whirring, engines rolling forward, forward, forward, and sirens in the distance.

Harold repeated his regret. "I said I'm sorry! I apologize!" The mayor's voice was even louder this time. As loud as he believed he could yell.

"You're a *dead* man!" The driver's voice boomed out the threat. The mayor couldn't believe what he was saying. He looked into the rearview at his face in doubt. Maybe he'd misunderstood. The noise was thunderous. He could have been mistaken. Harold looked once again at the man.

Then the driver repeated it with a boom, nodding his head. "You're a dead man, Mayor!"

Pyle's eyes widened. He rolled up his window.

He sped up and drove into the next lane to his right. The man followed and sped up onto his tail. The mayor pushed on the accelerator and slipped into the left lane, then again further into the adjacent left lane. The man did the same. The mayor sped up again, now cruising close to eighty-five miles per hour and swerved with less control to the farthest lane he could without entering the high-occupancy lane. The man copied his every move. Speeding up, changing lanes, speeding up again. The mayor began to panic. Without looking, he slipped quickly into the HOV lane, almost cutting off a woman who had a toddler in a child's seat in the back. The mayor quickly yanked his steering wheel in order to compensate but his Avalon drifted a little too far to the right and slipped luckily between two other cars. Traffic peeled away from him as he snaked to the left then the right. His head was beaded in a profuse sweat and it trickled into his wide eyes. He grappled at something, anything to wipe his brow. The man in the black car showed up again, this time on his passenger side, and rolled down his window. Harold did likewise. He'd talk this guy down. The man sneered with a cigarette hanging out of his glowering lips. Before Harold could say a word, the man bellowed out of the car, "Having fun, Mayor?"

The mayor realized this wasn't coincidence at all. He'd been set up. This goon was Pinzer's henchman. But Pyle stared far too long at Tweeter and didn't see the brake lights in front of him before it was too late.

Chapter 23

"Well, Georgie, you've been more than hospitable to me, and I've overstayed my welcome."

"Not at all, Helen. Don't be silly. I've enjoyed your company, actually. Since Bobby died, I don't get a lot of visitors." I thought back and realized I'd never gotten a lot of visitors even when he was alive but decided to keep it to myself.

"Well, Harold should be back soon, and I don't want to be late with his dinner. Thanks again, Georgie. Can we do it again sometime?"

"I'd love to."

"Then, till next time."

"Bye, Helen."

Helen got into her car and drove off.

Gangster slipped between my legs and ran outside. "You be careful, cat. You're coming back in again in a little bit so don't go too far!" My yelling sounded like some insane mother with a reckless toddler. I wondered if the neighbors ever heard me.

While cleaning up after our wine, my thoughts turned to Helen; having her stop by felt good in one sense and odd in another. She seemed very closed-off, cool. Even so, it was nice to have a friend, and I figured they came in all shapes, sizes, colors, and moods. I chalked off Helen's distant personality to acting the wife of a politician and felt a little sorry for her.

****

The digital display on my phone read: *Pyle, Harold.* When I picked up the phone, Helen sounded overly cool like when there's the sudden drop in temperature before a thunderstorm.

"What time is it?"

"I'm sorry to wake you. Oh, Georgette, call me back when you get up. It can wait until tomorrow."

I looked at the clock; it was just minutes before midnight. I knew if she was calling this late, it was because she felt the need to. "No, it's fine. What's up, Helen?"

"Oh, how do I say this?"

"What, Helen?" She had gotten my attention by sounding more worried about the situation than the time. "What is it?" I pressed her harder.

"It's Harold. It seems he's gotten himself into an accident, on the freeway, leaving Phoenix."

"Oh my God, Helen." I adjusted myself up into a sitting position. "Is he okay?"

"Well, that's just it, Georgie. The doctors say I should just wait to come down till tomorrow. He's not responding neurologically. He's stabilized. He's out of immediate danger, but he's not responding neurologically. That's what they said."

"What does it mean?"

"It means Harold is in some sort of coma."

"I'll be right over."

I pushed the cat out of the way and jumped up, pulled on a pair of jeans and a T-shirt. I called Vanessa, explained the situation, and told her to meet me at the Pyle's.

It hadn't been so many weeks since Bobby had

died, and I understood how fragile you become when submerged in a crisis. The crying, pulling yourself together, putting on a strong front, the eventual acquiescence into emotional upheaval, but mostly the crying, the crying, the crying.

****

The night had taken on a misty feel like one normally found around coastal settings. White, red, yellow, and green halos wrapped around stoplights and looked eerie against the dark sky. Each changing light blurred in the humid air; glowing orbs wrapped in undulating haze. Odd for the desert. I looked up at the moon and saw an expanding ring around it. A spring rain looked like it might be headed our way.

As I drove up to Helen's, only one fragmented light was lit, one that looked like it was sitting on her kitchen table, one with yellow, red, and blue glass. The light looked like a Picasso painting. I wondered if it was her writing lamp.

I could see two people inside as I made my way into her drive. Helen's car was visible in her garage, which was open and looked like a big, dark yawning mouth. When I got out of my car, a motion sensing light clicked on and flooded the front of her house and lawn washing everything in an unnatural glare. Knowing Helen by now, I figured this must have been one of Harold's ideas. Helen wouldn't dare add anything garish to her environment.

The meandering walkway of the house took on blackened hues between the night sky and the bright spotlight angling off bushes and trees and bending like a lurking monster in the dark. By the time I got to Helen's front door, she was standing inside it behind the screen.

"You really didn't have to come over, Georgie. It's way beyond the call of duty, really." She spoke quietly as she let me in.

"It's nothing." I grabbed her around the shoulders in an embrace and she held me tight while we stood in the open door. For the first time in a long time, someone held me longer than I'd held them. When we pulled away from each other, I could see Helen's eyes had been closed from the hug. She was opening them slowly.

"Come in. Have a glass of wine." She closed the door behind me, and I heard someone getting another glass from the cupboard and heard the glug of wine being poured into it.

"This is becoming a habit." The voice, the unmistakable voice, offered commentary to the evening.

"Hi, Van," I said.

"Hey. Helen and I decided to partake. So, you're going to, too." She never asked permission, only gave orders, but they were mostly kind orders.

"Line me up."

Helen seemed a bit out of kilter, which I'd expected she would. Her floral purse sat on top of the counter and was unlatched. There was an envelope sitting next to her purse with the flap side up, and when I walked in, she moved ahead of me and slid it into her bag, then latched it, and hung it off the back of her wooden chair.

"Here." Van handed me a glass.

"How'd you get here? I didn't see your car."

"I walked. Felt like I could use the fresh air."

"Looks like rain."

"Wouldn't rain be a sign from the gods showing they cared about the little town of Sunnydale."

We fell in around the table. They took their respective seats, and I pulled out an unclaimed chair and sat down in front of my wine glass.

"Hear anything more, Helen?" I lifted my glass and took a sip.

"No. I've been waiting. Waiting and writing. This seems so familiar. Like when Bobby..." Her thought trailed off and she looked out the window onto some remembered past within the arms of the black scene outside.

Van and I made an unnoticeable exchange.

"You just don't worry. Sometimes head injuries are like that." Vanessa spoke with authority. "Miraculous things have happened. The brain is an amazing piece of machinery. Try not to worry."

"Oh, I'm not worried." She looked in our direction again. "More concerned than worried."

We waited for her to continue.

"I'm tossed. Tossed between him dying and, oh, God, save my soul for saying this." Her hands came up to cover her mouth. "And me living." She covered her eyes and wept.

What do you say at a confessional? Well, I'd never been much of a churchgoer, that's for sure! But I knew although you might beg God for forgiveness, He might not always grant it. I couldn't believe what I was hearing. Vanessa said something like, "There, there. You're just upset."

But then the words just fell out of my mouth. I'd neither the inclination nor the desire to hold them back and it was only after I'd spoken, I realized how harsh they sounded.

"If it's so bad, Helen, why don't you just get a divorce?" I was quick to anger and my chin tightened. I could tell it was quivering.

They both looked at me stunned. Vanessa particularly. I went on anyway. "Well really, Van, good grief. You and I both know things can get bad, but I never wished Bobby *dead*, not once. Did you?" Even as I spoke the words, my thoughts whipped back to mine and Bobby's last fight, our last night. Anger can make a person wish the worst.

"Georgie, quiet."

"Well, did you?" My eyes glared at Vanessa, if for no other reason but some misplaced validation for this worst of human emotions. Even so, I turned my ire back to Helen and went on. "You should be ashamed of yourself, Helen, for even thinking something like that, let alone saying it. I thought we were here to console you, not to devise some catch net in hopes of Harold's passing. And you, Van, to accept this as "okay" is beyond my sense of understanding." I paused, but only for a beat, and started up again.

"Did you ever wish Bobby were dead during your divorce?" I looked at her, demanding an answer.

"You want to go at this now?"

My response was to stare her down.

"Okay, okay. Let's do it. Yes! There, I said it. I wished he were dead instead of with another woman. Yes." Her face softened and looked at Helen. "Yes, damn you, Georgette. I'm so ashamed of it now. When he did die, all I could think was I'd brought it on somehow. I know it's ridiculous, but…"

Then Helen chimed in. "How did this evening get to be about the two of you?" She stood and when she did, her chair scuffed noisily on the tile floor. "How dare you judge me?" She glared at me. "How dare you."

She turned her wrath on Vanessa. "Bob was a good man. You two had been having trouble for a long time, Vanessa. Why do you think you had the right to wish him dead? He was a good man. Honest. Caring. Gentle. I knew a man like him once."

We both looked up as she continued her tirade.

"Yes, after I was married to Harold. We had an affair, a one-night stand. It all happened so suddenly and sweetly. I told Harold, asked him for a divorce." When she said 'divorce,' she looked at me sternly. "He wouldn't hear of it!" Her arms flew up. "I thought it was my way out. Then, Harold started laying down laws, new laws. I 'must be home by three in the afternoon and I wasn't to go out with my girlfriends.' They're all gone now. Until you two."

As she continued, Vanessa sat back in her chair and crossed her arms. Her mouth had dropped slightly into what I took as her disbelief in Helen's sudden burst of backbone.

"So, don't either one of you decide what you think is right and wrong for Helen. Little Miss Helen Pyle can make her own decisions. Don't think otherwise." She sat stiffly and abruptly back into her seat. Her arms, like her mood, were crossed. "Now, I think it's time you both leave. I'm up early tomorrow to go to Phoenix."

Apologizing at this point would have seemed sleazy, teenage. I pushed my chair in under the table and smacked Vanessa on the arm. She seemed to be taking too long to stand.

"Helen, honestly, I'm sorry." Vanessa said it as sincerely as she could under the circumstances. I knew she was trying to think of how bad Helen was feeling but Helen's words still sounded cheap.

"Van, come on." I hit her arm again. This time she moved.

Outside, the night had become windy while we sat inside discussing life and death and our husbands. You could feel the mugginess wrap around your skin like a wetsuit. The air smelled of creosote and honeysuckle. It smelled as though someone left a sprinkler on a dry, dusty road. I could almost taste mud pie.

We were definitely in for some bad weather.

Chapter 24

The next night ended like a bad dream, with monsters and spiders, a horrible recurring nightmare. But this time it was worse, much, much worse.

It had been pissing down rain ever since around seven in the morning. Roads were flooded and there had been a rumor they might even close the school until it cleared up a bit.

The diner was closed, and Vanessa went AWOL.

Everyone was looking for her. I'd called her house, Roberta, the diner—the only places Vanessa seemed to frequent these days—and she was nowhere; it was like she'd vanished. I even called Helen. But after the phone rang and rang, I remembered she had planned to go see Harold in Phoenix. When Roberta got my call, it must have upset her because she started on a search of her own. José called me in the morning, too, and I told him if he saw her anywhere to tell her to call. He was going in to check on the garden and he said if she came by, he would relay the message.

The morning sun lifted high in the sky and began its descent. By then, around two o'clock, my inner voice began to tell me things I didn't want to hear.

Something is wrong! Go to her house, start walking the streets calling her name, like you would if you lost Gangster. Just do something!

When I drove up, Roberta's car was already parked

in her driveway. I pulled up next to it and, as I was exiting the car, she came out of the kitchen door walking slowly toward me. She was shaking her head and looking down at her feet. My heart started to pound.

Roberta leaned against the car. "She's not here."

"Oh, Christ, Roberta. You scared me, shakin' your head and all. I didn't know what to think."

"Sorry," Roberta answered curtly. She never talked kindly to me.

"Well, I guess we better keep lookin', huh?"

"She'll turn up."

"She's never been gone this long without telling someone."

Roberta sneered at my whining voice. "You've known her now for how long? And you're telling me, her *daughter*, she's never done this before. Is *that* it, Georgette?" Hatred dripped from her mouth.

"I didn't, I didn't mean…" My head was shaking, and I was trying to think up something to say.

She stood up straight and seemed to be looking down on me.

She said, "If I hear from her, I'll tell her you've been looking for her." I stepped out of her way as she walked between her car and me. She opened it and got in.

As I stood by the driveway, I realized I'd lulled myself into believing Roberta was possibly accepting me but I had forgotten how deeply the divorce cut her. I was the other woman, deeply embedded in her mother's life, her life. The hum of her motor buzzed in the background of my thoughts. She pushed her horn, just once, short. It jolted me from my thoughts. My car blocked her. I hurried to get in and I pulled out far enough for her to pull out in front of me. She did and drove off.

****

By three, the diner looked closed, which it was. Lights off, no cars in front, lifeless. José was out in the back on his knees, yanking out weeds and busily working in the soil.

"Seen Vanessa?" He jerked when I spoke. I'd startled him.

"Oh, Mrs. Carlisle, you scared me."

"Sorry, José. Has Vanessa been by?"

"Haven't seen her." He looked around out to the north, then east, then south.

"What's up, José?"

"Oh, a man was walking around here earlier. I didn't recognize him."

"What did he look like?"

"Big. I didn't get a good look at him. Like I said, I didn't recognize him. He was wearing dark sunglasses. He was only here for just a second. I saw him over there." José pointed to the side of the diner. "But then he was gone." Sweat poured down José's face and he wiped it with the upper part of his sleeve. "Maybe he wanted to eat."

We both started to look around then, like the man might show up again.

"Well, if you see Vanessa will you tell her to call me, José? I'm starting to worry a little."

"Okay, Mrs. Carlisle." He dropped to his knees again and busily picked leafy vegetables and put them in his basket.

****

It wasn't so unusual for one of us, me, or Vanessa, to show up the evening before we opened for the week after our days off. Driving in, the moon was cresting over the mountains in the distance and yet the sun was still peeking low along the hills in the opposite horizon. I was gazing out the driver's side window enjoying the sunset when I heard another car approaching me fast, it sounded like the driver was gunning it. Next thing I see is this truck coming straight for me and honking its horn. We both swerved out of each other's lane. I was only half a block from the diner and nearly got into an accident. It felt like my biorhythms were out of whack.

When I pulled up, Roberta's car was parked outside the diner. She and I seemed to be on the same wavelength and mission to find her mother. The restaurant's motion detector blinked and clicked on when I stepped out of my car. I unlocked the door and heard a shuffle in the kitchen.

"Vanessa!" I called out. "Vanessa!" I called out again a little louder.

"Help me." The words sounded puny.

My purse dropped where I stood and I ran toward the voice, a woman's voice. The kitchen was upended. By the door, the mixer hung from the outlet off the counter and onto the floor; a rack was pulled part way out of the wall and hung from one screw. Aprons were strewn around, the knife holder tipped over, and there was blood behind the center island on a wall smeared down below the line of my sight.

I screamed, "Vanessa!" and ran around to help.

But it wasn't Vanessa, it was Roberta was lying on the floor in an expanding pool of blood.

"Oh my God!" I ran to the phone and called nine-one-one. After relaying information to the operator, I grabbed an apron and rushed over to Roberta with it. Pressing the cloth firmly into the wound in her stomach, I tried to speak calmly and quietly. Our eyes connected and she looked sweet and peaceful.

"Georgie, I…"

"Roberta, don't talk. Stay real quiet, honey. You need to keep your heart calm; you mustn't lose any more blood. The paramedics will be here in a second. Shh." As I finished, we could hear sirens in the distance approaching rapidly and come to a sliding stop on the gravel outside the diner. The door opened. I looked toward the sound then back to Roberta. She smiled at me and then closed her eyes.

"In here. Hurry!"

The EMTs worked fast and furiously. I stayed back against a wall and watched as they administered a syringe full of coagulant into her hip, blood, and fluids into her vein, and pressed an oxygen mask onto her face. They lifted her onto the gurney, put her into the ambulance, and drove off blaring urgently. I got lost in the waning sound as it sped away.

Then I heard Willy say quietly to another officer. "We need to call the coroner and the crime scene unit. This one didn't make it."

"What?" His words surfaced like a shark's fin in the water.

"You need to stay back, Mrs. Carlisle." He held his arms up to block me from the back door where he stood.

"What is it? What is it, Willy?" He dropped his head.

"Let me by."

"Mrs. Carlisle, you can't go back there. You shouldn't. It's a crime scene now. We can't have you destroy possible evidence, understand?"

"Willy." He knew I was serious.

"Look from the door. Don't contaminate the evidence, Georgette. It's important." I walked by him to the opening of the door. When I looked out, my heart started to race, and my legs felt weak and shaky. I heard my own frail voice call out to Willy, "No. Oh, no. No, God, no."

Only his body lay there. It wasn't really him anymore. The blood pooled down the ramp and into the dirt. It looked like water, dark water, surrounding him as it bled off and into his garden. He looked so small, and he had fallen in a contorted position making his body appear disjointed and appear as if seen through a prism into a distorted version of reality.

The doorjamb caught my body as I slid down the door until I reached the floor. My hands covered my face.

"Mrs. Carlisle, there's nothing you could've done."

Then he said something about rigor and that at least an hour had gone by. The night seemed unending but only fifteen minutes had passed since I'd walked through the door. My instincts had been right. My worries were met face-to-face with horror. Roberta might not make it. She'd been shot high in the stomach. Now this. Where was Vanessa? How could I explain to her what had happened? How could I tell her José had been killed?

Chapter 25

The hospital buzzed with doctors and nurses, police officers, and ambulances. The recovery room where Roberta slept felt miles away from the bustle. I'd given a police report of what little I knew. Told them about the previous vandalism—the first time they'd destroyed the garden, the day, the damage, and how we thought it was just the local juvenile element, nothing more.

We stood close to the emergency entrance while I laid out to a police officer the events as they had occurred over the past couple of weeks. As we talked, a large van with "Coroner" lettered across its hind doors backed up to the large double doors of the emergency entrance. The medics pulled out a person on a gurney covered from head-to-toe under a blue cotton sheet. When they lowered him, a wheel on the gurney caught on one of the medic's shoes. The gurney jerked into place but doing so jostled the body. His hand fell out from under the sheet and it was then it finally struck me, José was dead. His hand was proof. I gasped and covered my eyes. The officer walked over and gently put José's hand back under the cover. He said something to the medics, who quickly looked over at me, then focused on the officer's face and shook their heads apologetically.

I wondered what they were going to tell José's

wife. Her life would be severed.

****

She looked like an angel, like Bobby, as she lay there unconscious. Memories flooded me about her. The screaming match she had with him before the divorce. She didn't realize I was in Bobby's hotel bathroom with him when she happened by. She carried on solid before Bobby could get a word in edgewise. When he did, he just said, "Sorry, honey. Someday you'll understand, or not." She slammed the door hard when she left. He was dreadfully sad. The divorce was finalized the following week. Roberta showed up with her mother at the hearing. Bobby, the petitioner, took the stand and was asked if there was any hope for reconciliation. After he responded *no*, Roberta stood up and called her father a coward. He looked at me squarely in the eyes as if he'd lost all hope. I shook my head because I didn't know what to do.

"Roberta," he said, "Roberta, honey, this is not about you." The court recorder kept typing the words. The whole thing was public record.

And when they asked Vanessa if she'd like to respond, she only said, "Forty-five years." She got up and walked out of our lives. I took his hand when he got down from the witness stand. He was shaking like a leaf.

The next time we heard from Roberta, two years later, her mother had been admitted to the oncology ward of Las Vegas General Hospital for breast cancer. After a year of chemo and radiation therapy, Vanessa was given a clean bill of health. Bobby helped out the best he could. He visited her in the hospital twice and went over to Rick and Roberta's when all seemed lost.

But thanks to the good Lord above, she lived. To that, as far as the doctors were concerned, so would Roberta, now.

The blood pressure monitor dinged every three minutes for three hours and by ten thirty in the evening, Vanessa was still missing in action. *Ding.* An ICU nurse came in and checked Roberta's vitals. *Ding.* An orderly came in and replaced a bag of blood. *Ding.*

My mind was bouncing around like a bullet shot off in a lead barrel when the frantic yet familiar voice of Vanessa as she spoke to the nurse at the station outside Roberta's room. "Banner, Carlisle-Banner, Roberta Carlisle-Banner. What room is she in?" The nurse said something that pissed her off. "I'm her mother!" I stood up to go to the door and call Vanessa over. But she was headed in before I could cross the room.

"Oh my God. Oh my God."

"She's okay, Van. She's gonna make it." I tried to calm her down, but she'd have nothing of it. It seemed she blamed herself.

"Roberta, my baby. Oh, my Lord, please. Oh, my God, please. Lord, please." I was miles away from the two of them as I stood behind Vanessa. The nurse must have alerted the resident-on-staff because he came in only moments after she arrived.

"Mrs. Carlisle?"

"Yes." Her voice sounded gritty and her face was tight.

"Mrs. Carlisle, your daughter lost a lot of blood."

Vanessa's hand rose up to her mouth and she started to cry.

"She's stable right now and has been for a good

hour. She's doing remarkably well for the injury she's sustained."

"What happened?"

"Well, she received a gunshot wound to the left side of her stomach and she's had surgery. We've stopped the bleeding and she's recovering just like she should. She's going to be fine, but she needs rest to build her strength. We're checking on her every half hour. She's recovering nicely. She'll be fine." He was very considerate and kept repeating how well Roberta was doing.

Vanessa sat in the chair I'd been filling in her absence, holding her daughter's hand, the one I'd held, and staring into her face. I stood behind her and watched the two sit silently together. Mother and daughter. When I left the room, Vanessa hadn't even noticed.

****

At one o'clock in the morning, the phone rang. I scrambled to it. "Hello."

"Georgie, it's me, Van."

"Oh, hi, hon. How's Roberta doing?"

"She's doing better, I think."

"Thank God, Van. Thank God."

"Yeah." She paused.

"Van?"

"Oh, Willy came by after you left. I didn't know you'd gone, Georgie."

"You two needed to be alone. I didn't want to disturb you by saying I was leaving." She sniffled a little, and I realized she was crying.

"I can come back, Van. Do you want me to come back?"

****

Using my fingers as a comb, I tried to fix my hair as I climbed from the car in the hospital parking lot. My breath smelled like hell, so I stuffed a piece of cinnamon gum in my mouth and chewed.

She looked used up but smiled at me anyway when I walked into the room again.

I whispered. "How's she doin'?"

"She's great." She paused again. So, I pulled up a chair to sit next to Van.

"She's a strong girl, Van. She's gonna come out of this with shining colors, you just see." Van smiled at me and tears filled her eyes. She covered her face.

"It's all I've done tonight, you know, cry like this."

"Hey. It's understandable. You cry. Cry good and hard if you want; I've been doing my fair share."

"Willy told me, Georgie." Her eyes were wet and focused deep into mine. "He told me everything. He told me if you hadn't…"

"Shh…" I stopped her with my hand up to her. I knew what she meant.

"Did he tell you about José?" Her head nodded slowly. "If I'd only gotten there a little sooner, Van, maybe…"

My strength slipped away without a care; I couldn't contain my sorrow. She pulled me into her, and we sat for a long time, just consoling each other. We sat there just holding each other, holding each other up.

Chapter 26

"This is what we know so far, Mrs. Carlisle," Willy spoke pointedly without giving me too much information, "the lock on the desk drawer in your office was pried open, maybe with a crow bar, and Vanessa Carlisle's gun was the weapon involved. We suspect José and Roberta both interrupted a burglary—José first, then Roberta, after they'd shot José."

"Our gun?"

"Well, it's registered to Vanessa, Georgette. Why do you say our gun?"

"She bought it for us to use, you know, just in case." I couldn't believe what Willy was telling me. Vanessa would never forgive herself.

"In case of what?"

"She got spooked one day at the diner and bought it a couple days later."

"Spooked by what, Georgette?"

"Some big, ugly guy at the restaurant. He said some things to her that made her a little nervous. I can't remember exactly."

"She bought it then?"

"Well, actually, I think it was the day the vandals broke into the stores down the strip from us. The kids, remember?"

"Mm-hmm. Well, Georgette, if you can think of anything else, anything at all that seems a little odd or out of the ordinary, call me, okay? Anytime, you hear?"

"I will." I got up to go and just as I stood, I said. "Oh, Willy, this whole thing has been so awful. I keep replaying things in my head about the day, like a tape recorder, over and over." We were leaving the interview room.

"Georgette, I think it'll be a long time before anyone gets over this. It's affected the entire town."

"Poor José."

"I know. Try not to think about it. Don't 'what-if' yourself. It'll make you crazy."

"That's just it, Willy. I think what if I'd gotten there earlier, would José still be alive? And then I think what if I'd gotten in that accident, would Roberta…"

"What accident?" We were coming into the police station lobby and I was watching my feet. The floor was always a mess there for one reason or another.

"Oh, I nearly went head-on into an SUV about a block from the restaurant. I wasn't paying attention and crossed over the center line. If I'd hit the other car, Willy, Roberta would be dead, too. I just can't shake the thoughts out of my head anymore. They keep me up at night."

"Try not to think about it. I know it's not easy but try to soothe your mind. Think about good things. Well, Georgette, I have to get back to work. Thanks for coming in. Take care."

"Bye, Willy."

****

Vanessa couldn't believe the smell, or the assortment of smells, permeating the police station—coffee brewing, vomit, smoke, alcohol, body odor—all emanating from a variety of suspects, offenders, and a stained coffee pot on the sergeant's desk one facing the double glass doors. She nearly turned around and walked out but stopped herself. She yanked at her jacket's hem and coughed slightly, then walked nervously up to the man sitting behind the desk. She didn't recognize him.

"My name is Vanessa Carlisle. I'm here to see Willy, Officer Willard Cleary, please."

"Carlisle?"

"Yes. Vanessa Carlisle."

"Just a minute, please." He picked up the phone and dialed an extension. "Willy, a Vanessa Carlisle is here, Mmm-hmm, will do.

"He says he'll be out in just a minute and to have a seat."

She looked around at the available chairs in the lobby, one next to a scruffy-looking man with stained and tattered clothing who was rambling loudly about the dogs at the racetrack. There was another next to a pierced and tattooed, young, pregnant girl who wore handcuffs sitting with an officer who was taking notes, and another one in between a whirring pop machine and a decent enough-looking young man filling out something on a clipboard. She took a seat and held her purse tightly on her lap. Her widening hips barely fit into the metal frame of the chair and made telltale dents where it pressed into her. Wanting to rest her hands by her sides in order to hide her legs would mean relinquishing the tight grip she held on her purse. Vanity lost out and she only looked back down once at her bulging thighs. On the floor under her feet was a sticky, distorted circle of spilled cola. She tried to place her feet around it but found it futile and relinquished to placing them smack in the center with her feet close together.

Only a moment passed when Willy showed up. She had to wrench herself free from the chair. It insisted on remaining attached to her buttocks and did momentarily then dropped and clanked noisily against the tile floor when it landed. She straightened her pants and walked up to Willy to shake his hand. Whatever slime she'd picked up on her shoes was sticking to the floor and made a sucking noise each time she stepped.

"Mrs. Carlisle." He grabbed her extended hand.

"Please, Willy, call me by my name. How long have we known each other? Is it twenty some years now?"

"Vanessa."

"That's better." They let go of each other's hands.

"Come with me. We can talk somewhere a little more private." He led her through the lobby and down a hall of windowed offices—some with two and three desks, some with only one—into one with mini blinds and a solid door with a conference table.

"Have a seat." He twisted the control to close the blinds. "Would you like something to drink? Coffee?"

"A glass of water would be great."

He walked out and closed the door part way. She wondered why he would shut the mini blinds. Did he think she would act out or cry? She felt her body tense and begin to quiver. No sooner did her fears begin to grip her than Willy walked back in. She jumped when he spoke.

"Here we go...oh, I'm sorry, Vanessa. I didn't mean to startle you." He placed the water on the table by her.

"I always forget how nervous people get in this place. I'm used to it, of course. But I remember a time when I wasn't. You okay?"

"Sure, Willy. Thanks." She slid the paper cup closer and held it firmly with both hands. After she was sure her hands wouldn't shake, she lifted the cup and took a long gulp. Willy watched her as he sat down in the chair facing her. "That's better. I'll be fine. I'm just, well, nervous, like you said."

"Don't worry about a thing. I just want to ask you a few questions about the day, you know, of the shooting."

Vanessa nodded anxiously.

"So, where were you that day?"

Vanessa shifted in her chair. "I had gone to a doctor's appointment in Flagstaff. It was at eleven in the morning and lasted the better part of the day. I think I left there around five thirty in the afternoon, around then. I stopped and had a quick dinner before heading back home." Willy started scribbling notes on a tablet of blue-lined yellow paper. "What's the doctor's name? I'll have to verify your times."

"Well, it wasn't really with a doctor." Willy looked up from the notes he was taking and set his pencil down when Vanessa hesitated. She could sense he wasn't happy with her response. "I was at the medical center at the university, having tests."

"I'll need someone's name to verify this, Vanessa. Can you tell me whom I can contact there?"

"The technician's name was Caroline Tagel. She pronounces her name, Carol-I-ne."

"Do you have a phone number I can call?"

"Not with me."

"Well, what department is she in?"

"Willy," she paused a moment and shook her head, "I'd rather not say."

"Vanessa, you can't withhold information from us."

"But it has nothing to do with the shootings."

"Vanessa." Willy grabbed both of her hands in his. "If this is embarrassing to you, I'll do everything in my power not to let it out if I can. But seeing as how this is a medical issue, you shouldn't have anything to worry about. We are very sensitive to this sort of thing. It comes up more than you'd think." He smiled sincerely at her. Vanessa smiled back and looked down again in order to drum up the courage to tell Willy about the cancer.

****

Willy stared as Vanessa walked through the double glass doors of the entrance and down the stairs outside. The sun was blazing down, and a dark shadow haloed the concrete sidewalk around her feet. He felt sorry for the woman he'd known almost as long as he'd lived here.

A meeting with Bill was next. He had more information today than yesterday and the pieces of the puzzle were slowly beginning to paint a picture of the night in question. He felt they were only steps behind the killer. They needed to find a shoe one to match the imprint picked up from the crime scene, and a man driving an SUV, the same SUV Georgette saw driving away before she showed up at the diner and found Roberta.

He'd had mixed feelings about Georgette, the other woman, the mistress, those sorts of thoughts, but saving

Roberta seemed to clear the slate for her. If she hadn't shown up, Roberta would be dead now. As Vanessa walked out of view, he wondered if she knew.

Chapter 27

Exactly one week after the autopsy, José was shipped where he wanted to be buried. Maria escorted his body in the hearse to the airport and then to Mexico. His family welcomed her sadly. His funeral mass, the burial, and José's *fiesta de vida* continued for the better part of an entire morning, afternoon, and evening. The large family celebrated him and the memory of him.

That same day, Vanessa and I held a quiet ceremony in the garden behind our diner. We were standing by a special pepper patch of José's. In it, we constructed a cross where we hung photos of José. One was of José and Bobby as they dug out a spot for the very patch where we now stood. His eyes were smiling, and his denim overalls were covered in dirt. Bobby stood behind him like a proud father as José pointed at a pouch of seeds in his hand. There was a wedding photo of him and Maria, and one of him selling vegetables to a tourist. Others covered every inch of the white wooden cross, just as representative of José and his sweet demeanor.

Days before the ceremony for José, we had told several of our customers about the service we intended to have and explained the circumstances around his death.

People can be so kind, strangers even, in times of desperation.

Vanessa began to read from the Bible, a passage from the Book of Esther. "And when these days were expired…"

But a man stopped her when he called out gently from over by the garden gate. We turned to look and saw Arnie standing under the garden's arch. We could only see just behind him. There were a few regulars from the restaurant. Vanessa's hand came up to her chest, her eyes got watery, but she beamed in gratitude at the crowd. My head dropped and I wept openly. I cared no less about letting people see me the way I was feeling at the moment. Nobody cared either. Arnie brought his wife and he let her, and Helen walk through in front of him and up to us. After that, a parade of friends showed up for José. Glenda came with the rest of our waitstaff, Mr. & Mrs. Rigger walked in gloomily and slowly, Detective Mark appeared behind them, then Willy, the EMTs, and Reverend Carney. The reverend carried a Bible and a box of money he'd collected from his parishioners for Maria. After that, I couldn't tell you. They just kept coming.

All I remember is the garden was full.

Then Vanessa continued, "And when these days were expired, the king made a feast unto all the people that were present in Shushan the palace, both unto great and small, seven days, in the court of the garden of the king's palace." She stopped and said, "Amen."

The crowd followed suit.

Even after so many years of living here, I still felt a little uncomfortable around the townsfolk. My strength came from doing something good for José, something Vanessa and I had not planned.

"Vanessa and I hope you'll all stay for a bite to eat

and to toast José." I looked at Vanessa for approval.

"Yes, please. It would be wonderful if you could join us."

****

Our little diner was packed. We opened up the doors to anyone who stopped by at no charge in honor of José. The menu was thrown together fast. As you might have suspected, we served fresh vegetables and salsa made from José's peppers and tomatoes, chips, queso, and bean dip. We drank red wine and raised our glasses in appreciation of our friend. We told stories, new and old, and remembered him. José filled so many people's hearts and wouldn't be forgotten by those he touched.

Chapter 28

It was always a little strange for me to be at Vanessa's house, but lately she'd been asking me to do little favors for her while she was at the hospital. I didn't mind and actually enjoyed helping out. She would ask me to do little things like take mail to the post office, run a deposit to the bank, or pick up a few groceries. Her key was under a rock in a potted plant on the back porch and I'd let myself in back there. The back door led straight into her kitchen. On the terracotta kitchen counter by the phone, she kept a stack of mail neatly against the wall, a note pad, and a cup of pens and pencils.

It was the day Roberta was being discharged from the hospital. I was bringing cookies and a few gifts by the house.

Plus, I was delivering some milk, eggs, and a few other staples she'd asked me to pick up for her, and I accidentally knocked the letters and bills and the cup with the pencils in it off the counter. I stepped over everything I'd knocked to the floor and set the bags of groceries down by the refrigerator, then went back to clean up my mess. Pens and pencils rolled everywhere, and papers scattered across the floor. I didn't mean to, but I noticed a bill from the university labs. Underneath the university labs envelope were other bills opened and without envelopes. A few bills had the words *oncology department* printed on the header and listed the patient's name: *Vanessa Carlisle*, and each one described the treatment received: *mammogram*, *biopsy*, and *result consultation*. My breath caught and somehow got tangled between my lungs and my heart. The fourth letter was still in an opened envelope and although I was incredibly curious, I wasn't about to pull out its contents and read it. I felt guilty enough for rustling through the open ones and seeing the confidential evidence Vanessa had kept to herself. Did Roberta know?

The day she got her consultation was the day of the break-in, the day of the shooting. That's how everyone referred to it anymore. No one wanted to say "the day José was killed, and the day Roberta almost died!" The day was dubbed '*the day of the shooting*' by nearly everyone in town. That's why we couldn't find Vanessa; she was learning about her own breast cancer.

I heard a car pull into the driveway and hurriedly stacked the bills together and put them back on the edge of the counter. When I walked out, she was already helping Roberta from the passenger side.

"Do you need help?"

"She's doing so well, Georgie, really well!" She sounded like a new mother watching her toddler learn how to walk.

"Why, yes, she is."

"Will you two stop? I'm fine. Please, Mother, stop coddling me."

Roberta sounded like her old self again and was slapping at her mother's hands, which were trying to help. It appeared at no time could Vanessa do the right thing for her daughter. Then, I had a brief notion the discharge of this patient came about more out of concern for the nurses than for Roberta's recovery, but like I said, it was a fleeting thought. Vanessa had successfully helped her out all the way by then and Roberta was standing, no wait, leaning against the car. She was holding her side and wincing.

"She sure sounds spunky."

"I'm he-ere. I can hear you both talking." The old Roberta was back with a few bumps and bruises, but she was back.

"You'll need help for a while. You let your mother help you. I have some more things in my car. I'll see you both inside."

****

Roberta was sitting at the kitchen table when I came back in, and Vanessa was putting on a strong front for her daughter. She had hot water simmering on the stove for tea and she had washed a couple of dusty teacups from the cupboard.

"Want some?" Vanessa looked at me and held up a teacup.

"Oh, no, Van. Thanks though. I have to get back home. Tomorrow will be the first day back at the diner and I have a few things I need to do before we get busy again."

I inadvertently looked at her chest to see if I could see anything. I don't know what I was thinking and when Vanessa saw me, she quickly turned her back toward me and faced the kitchen sink. Covering for what had just happened I said, "Roberta, there are cookies in this bag and, in this one, a few books and things. Van, I put a casserole in your refrigerator so you won't have to cook tonight." I looked back to Roberta.

"You can go through this stuff when you get comfortable, or hungry!" I laughed and she laughed with me. The teapot began to whistle, and Van got a couple of bags of chamomile tea and placed one in each cup.

"Well, I'd better get. Take care, y'all."

"Wait, Georgie," Roberta moved as if she was going to get up.

"Don't get up. What is it, honey?" I walked over to where she was sitting, and she held out her hand to shake mine.

"Are we business partners all of the sudden or did I miss something?" I knew she was trying to reach out, trying to say thank you.

So, I grabbed her one hand in both of mine and leaned into her, kissed the side of her face, and whispered in her ear, "I'm so very happy you're all right." When I pulled back from being there longer than what a person would think is normal, she had tears in her eyes. "Don't you start that, you hear? If you do, I will, and I don't want to! So, stop it!" But it was too late. Roberta was full-on crying by now and laughing at the same time. So, I did stupid things in front of her. I clog-danced and all of me wiggled and jiggled and stomped, to make her laugh more, which made her gut ache, which made her laugh more, then act mad at me, and finally stop crying. Vanessa was watching the whole thing as she leaned against the counter behind her.

"If she busts a suture it'll be your fault, Georgette."

"Yeah, yeah, if…" I turned to Vanessa, winked at her, said my goodbyes again, and began to walk out.

"Georgette." Vanessa walked to the edge of the

counter where I stood and put her hand on the stack of bills, looked at me, and slid the bills against the wall. My eyes dropped to her hand and followed her movement. Our eyes met. Hers told me she knew I'd seen something she didn't want anyone to know. She gave her head a tilt toward her daughter and widened her eyes with fear. "Thanks, honey, for everything." My head shook up and down in agreement, not for the thanks but to let her know her secret was safe.

I was about to my car and nearly ready to cry when Vanessa ran out to stop me.

"Georgie, wait up." When she got to me, she was very upset. She'd been hiding it well inside the house. "She still can't remember what happened."

"Anything?"

"Nope. The doctors said it could last a week or a year."

"Well, let's hope it's sooner than later. Is she going to see anyone?"

"I think so but she's not sure."

****

I was amazed at the amount of e-mail messages I'd gotten without having many friends and having absolutely no living family. Yet daily I'd get notification of millions of dollars being held in some fictionalized account for me, a Viagra promotional, or another online catalog advertisement. I'd deleted them all after reading everything in its entirety. Loneliness was my best friend lately. I blamed my ennui on not working for the past week and, of course, I still missed Bobby terribly. I got up to go to the bathroom and as soon as I sat down, I heard the telltale ding of mail arriving in my inbox. After washing my hands and face and brushing my teeth, I decided to see what it was.

It was a letter from RobCarBan@aol.com. I double-clicked it.

Dear Georgette,

Thanks for everything. I know you've been carrying the load for Mother these past few days. We both appreciate how much you've helped out. Thanks for the food too! The casserole was very tasty, but I preferred the cookies. I should get shot more often. Just kidding.

I'm being chicken by telling you this in an e-mail. I should call and talk to you personally, but I'm sorry, I just can't. Thank you also for the wonderful gifts. I love the dream journal and writing materials. I've already started jotting down some of my thoughts about things, life, you know?

But especially, Georgette, thank you for giving me Dad's "favorite" pen and the lovely note you wrote me. I'm deeply touched by this, you don't know how much, honestly. You've been more than a friend, Georgie, much, much more.

Profoundly, Roberta.

I wrote back,

Thank you, one million times, Roberta. Love, G.

Chapter 29

She looked in the closet on what used to be Harold's side. Only a few slacks hanging and shirts neatly pressed and buttoned at the top like he asked her to do. All of the hangers pointed in the same direction toward the wall, and all of the shirts faced out toward the door of the closet—five dress shirts in total, five pairs of slacks. His seersucker suit had been sent back from the hospital, and his luggage sent back from the highway patrol. They deemed the collision an accident and didn't need to investigate further or hold in evidence any of Harold's belongings ones found in his crumpled vehicle. The bag was unopened and had remained until until this morning, the morning she decided to build up her courage and go through Harold's things. That's what wives do when husbands die. She felt she should cry but had not. Guilt outweighed her sadness. She wondered how Georgette had handled this process. She knew Bob and Georgette had experienced what only a few lucky married couples experience together, a caring, loving life, much different than hers and Harold's. Oh, sure, Bob and Georgette had troubles now and again, she knew for a fact, but nothing they hadn't survived.

She pulled out his ten pieces of clothing and laid them on top of the neatly made bedspread. One by one, she unbuttoned the collars of the shirts and one by one she folded them each and laid them properly in a box marked *Thrift Store*. After which she pulled Harold's piece of black and gray paisley luggage up onto the bed and opened the lock. It smelled like Harold. She held her breath before opening it. After talking herself into it, she lifted the lid and let it fall back onto the bed. The turquoise suit was squashed inside it to fit, along with a pair of cowboy boots, his briefs, a zippered bag with his grooming items inside, and a leather folder he carried with him when he went to and from his office at the courthouse. She set it aside and began pulling out and folding the clothing, placing them all in the box intended for the thrift store as well.

Helen unzipped his carryall and pulled out his shaver, shaving gel, toothpaste, and toothbrush. She let her thumb run up and down the bristles a couple of times and she gazed up and out the small window. She realized then she was on her own. No more Harold.

The thought of changing her name back to her maiden name crossed her mind but it was fleeting. Her timing needed to be just right. Changing her name too soon would make eyebrows raise and people whisper. She needed to give herself some room before making the change. She was unsure of the proper amount of time to do something of this nature, so she decided she'd have to refer to an etiquette manual. but wondered, *do they address such things*?

She looked back down to the bag, a hairbrush, cologne, Preparation H. She huffed in amusement when she pulled it out. Helen walked into the bathroom for the waste bucket, returned, and loaded it with Harold's toiletry items. She then walked back and put the bucket back in its place by the toilet. She looked at herself in the mirror and checked her teeth, opened the medicine cabinet, pulled out her toothbrush, filled it with a striped paste, and began brushing. She stared blankly into the mirror, spat, and rinsed, then pulled her hair back in a clip and washed her face. She wiped off the mirror where toothpaste had speckled it, wiped down the sink, and noticed how perfectly fresh the house smelled sans Harold. Even though Harold was a prig, he still passed gas like a lumberjack. Something Helen had grown to despise over the years. The lavender cleaner she used for the bathroom scented the air and she breathed it in deeply.

She rezipped his luggage and put it back into the darkest corner of the closet. She was about to turn off the light and close the door when she decided to take the piece of luggage back out and store it in the garage where it would take up less space. She decided she would put it on a high shelf inside one of the storage bins where Harold kept his fishing gear.

She lugged the piece out of the bedroom through the hall into the kitchen, through the laundry room, and out into the garage. She flicked on the light switch and saw only her car. She had insisted on something nice this time. She didn't want to buy used, she wanted a new car and had to fight Harold to get it. Her last winning pitch was the argument where she told him a mayor's wife should reflect her husband's success. She played to his ego. After that, Harold allowed her to buy the a classy SUV. Today, the car was four years old.

Helen smiled. She'd fought and won. Then she thought how many times she could've won if she'd only been stronger, fought harder. Then she thought how many things she'd wanted and hadn't fought for at all.

Her smile dissipated and she moved through the door toward the storage bin and placed the piece of paisley luggage on the floor to get a stepladder.

After unlocking the bin, she opened and angled the ladder into place, picked up the empty bag and carried it up the stairs arm-down. She hoisted the bag up onto her shoulder and again up to the top shelf inside the bin and slid it back, but it stopped short, not allowing enough room to close the doors. It hung over the edge a good three inches she suspected.

She pulled the bag out and held it in her hand. A good twelve inches shorter than the uppermost top of the cabinet, Helen popped up onto her toes and moved her hand to feel around for whatever had blocked Harold's bag. She blindly patted until she felt something she could make out as a thin, flat item.

Pulling the thing forward, she inched it forward with the tips of her fingertips until she finally got it to a point where she could slide it out far enough onto the ledge to lift it by pinching it between her index finger and thumb.

As she pulled it closer to her head, she saw it was a black attaché with the insignia CII.

She pulled it off and then replaced the luggage she'd been holding into its spot. It fit nicely now.

When she got down from the ladder, she closed and locked the bin once again. She then walked back into her house, looking at the latched attaché she'd found.

****

Vanessa and I drove to Helen's together. When we got there, we were all sad smiles and baked goods. I brought a pie and Van brought lasagna; we both brought sympathy cards and wanted to sit with her and console her the best we knew how. But Helen was beyond consoling. She was beyond everything. She seemed distant and cold. This woman who had once been our friend now treated us like her and Harold's constituency, mere voters. Standing in the doorway, she said she didn't have a lot of time. She needed to organize the memorial service, answer a few phone calls. Although she said she appreciated the gesture, the day was running short and she'd have to ask us over again on another day soon. We took it she was grieving, albeit differently than how *we* might have expected and when she closed the door, we turned and stared at each other but then walked back to the car, and left.

****

After the initial jolt of finding Harold's incriminating documents, Helen was enraged. Her name would be mud around Sunnydale; she'd be the laughingstock of the community along with Harold, but Harold could hide in the confines deep inside the earth. She'd have to bear his misconduct, the underhandedness of his ambition, the ensuing damage upon people and property, the lies, deceit, and crime involved. She'd feel the brunt of his burden. By then it was late in the afternoon and as the sun began its decline in the western sky, she'd settled into her fourth scotch. She'd kept the bottle close at hand for her fifth and possibly sixth if she could stand the imminent delirium brought about by the alcohol. She'd not have her name slandered. She'd refuse the attack from media attention. She'd not come forth until the police forced her hand if they were to force her hand at all. This was

Harold's doing, not hers, and she'd act as surprised at their findings as they would be.

Helen stumbled out to the back patio by the fire pit with the documents in hand. She teetered to a stack of logs, found kindling, layered it on the bottom of the pit's screen, and then added one single mesquite log to burn. She ignited the kindling after spritzing it with the lighter fluid they kept with the built-in barbecue. The building glow of the burning wood felt too hot in the warm evening air and she stepped back to the table under the umbrella where she'd left her drink and the guilty documents, contracts between Chariot International Incorporated all signed by a Zach Pinzer. Why hadn't she ever heard of this man before? But she knew all too well the answer to her questions. She wondered why Harold had such a sudden increase of generosity, the jewelry and gifts—guilt gifts, blood money, all of it.

The log had become fully engulfed in fire and popped into submission. Bits of hot ash spit from it as all its life was being burnt out. She pulled off the top page of the first document from the attaché and crumpled it into a ball in her fist. She walked slowly and deliberately toward the burning pit. Her future was now on the line. She wondered if she could flee before the fall of the axe. Run and hide. Helen thought of Seattle where no one knew her. Could she hide from the wide spreading arms of the media? She turned back to the table, walked over quickly, and grabbed her drink. She slugged back the sharp tonic, wiped her lips with her arm, and coughed bitterly. She turned now, stronger than before with her sweaty palm still tightly gripping the crumpled paper and walked steadily this time back to the fire.

Chapter 30

It was late in the evening just after the last party had left the diner. I was locking the door when I noticed a darkened car sitting alone in the front parking lot of the restaurant. I quickly turned the lock to secure the door. That's when a woman exited the vehicle and I realized who it was. After unbolting the lock, I opened the door for her.

"Helen, what are you doing here? I didn't recognize your car."

"Is Vanessa here?"

"Yes. What's goin' on?" I opened the door for her to enter and she walked in.

"I need to talk to the both of you."

"Oh, Helen, about the other night. I'm so sorry."

"Don't give it a second thought. Now, go get Vanessa, okay?"

She seemed firmer than the Helen I knew from before.

Of course, her husband had just died, and she was still in mourning. I went to the office where Vanessa was doing the books.

"Van?"

"Mm-hmm."

"Helen's here." Van looked up when I spoke. She pulled her readers from the bridge of her nose and let them loose on the chain around her neck.

"What's she want?"

"I don't know but she said she needs to speak with the both of us."

As I was speaking, Helen walked into the dining area. She was dressed nice enough but somehow had a disheveled look about her.

"Would you like a glass of wine, Helen?"

"I think I'd better not. Not until after I've said what I have to say to you."

"Okay, shoot, Helen." Vanessa seemed overly curt to me. She hadn't liked the way Helen had treated us when we tried to visit her.

We both slid into the booth opposite her. She looked out the window, holding a hanky in her hands, twining it over and over again. She rubbed just under her nose with a finger and I could see her hands were shaking.

"What's going on, Helen? You seem upset." Vanessa must have seen her shaking too.

"Well, Vanessa, I am upset. I don't know where to begin." We both looked on without saying anything and she started to unfold in front of us. "Oh God, what am I going to do?"

"Helen, how can we help if you don't tell us what's eatin' you?" She looked squarely into my eyes and spoke very methodically like she'd practiced it over and over in the mirror.

"I don't think Harold's accident was an accident at all. I think something underhanded was at play. I also think Harold had something to do with the vandalism down the strip and here, and the shooting." She sucked in a pocket of air and held her hands to her mouth.

Vanessa leaned forward upon Helen's confession.

"You think it was Harold?"

Helen shook her head and then spoke, "No, not Harold. Someone he was involved with."

"Who?"

"I'm not willing to say at this point, Vanessa, 'cause I'm not sure."

"My daughter almost died and you're not willing to say?"

I sank back into the corner of the booth when I felt Vanessa's rage, and Helen leaned against the back of hers.

"You don't understand. I'm not sure how Harold was involved. I just have a stinking sensation he was in deep, and completely out of his element."

"Helen, I have a question." Vanessa leaned back and let me talk. "What's led you to believe Harold was involved?"

"See, that's just it, Georgette. I was going through his things and by chance happened onto some documents, contracts. He'd hidden them on the top shelf of a storage cabinet in our garage. Well, these documents were all concerning land, businesses, buildings, and such here around Sunnydale. I know for a fact Harold had other business interests, he told me so. He just didn't say what they were. Honestly, when he brought home the deposit slip from his first commission check and it was over fifty thousand dollars, I was thrilled. I didn't realize it came from a shady deal."

"Where are these documents?" Vanessa was trying to contain her fury.

"They're still at the house. I thought maybe we could go over them together, the three of us. I'm not very business-minded and really need to know what you both think about them. Would you want to come over to my place? Tonight?"

****

The living room had papers all over the floor—contracts, credit card statements, and corresponding receipts, pay stubs, deposit slips, and phone logs—strewn across the floor, albeit in an orderly fashion. We all stood looking in from under the archway leading to the dining room.

"It's all there, all I could find at the house, anyway.

Who knows if there's more at his office. I haven't been by to pick up his things yet; they're letting me grieve." She rolled her eyes. "I was hoping you both could take a look at everything.

I've organized all of it in date order. It seemed the most logical thing to do. The contract lingo has me a little befuddled though. Would you mind?"

Vanessa and I entered the room like we had just found the Holy Grail, slowly, methodically, stepping over items carefully, staring at the volume of it all.

"I'll make some tea. Would tea be okay?"

Bold, brave Vanessa chimed in. "Honey, this is gonna take something stronger than tea."

Without a second thought, "Scotch it is." Helen had it close at hand. In the kitchen, we could hear ice drop into a tumbler, then another, then another, the gurgling sound of liquid coming out of the bottle, the bottom of each glass set back onto the counter, and then Helen's footsteps back toward us. By the time she returned, we were on the living room floor kneeling and reading the documents situated farthest to the left of the room. Like a book, we were reading a history of meetings and monies exchanged for services provided by the mayor to Chariot International Incorporated and all signed by Harold Pyle and a Zach Pinzer.

Vanessa reached for a glass with her gaze pasted onto the documents. I watched her as she read aloud, *"Pursuant to this agreement, the aforementioned Purchaser upon title exchanged for said Land will remit to the Intermediary Party a commission in the amount of $51,323.43."*

"Holy crap, that's a bunch of money! The land is the property just behind the diner. I thought the town of Sunnydale had been keeping the land preserved. This doesn't seem right. I don't know how Harold could've pulled this off without an uproar from the people here."

"You see, that's just it, Van. I remember him telling me it was all talk. Harold never really did anything about preserving the land because no one around here seemed to care too much one way or the other. He thought he could rally people for a preservation trust, but the idea sank before it even got started. Other things came up, bigger issues. People cared more about school levies, sales tax increases, and water issues. So, he dropped the ball. It's been town land from day one with no easements on it, no preservation classification. People assumed he'd followed through because he talked about it so often, but he hadn't. It was just town land sitting there, held in investment. But what I don't get is how he could sell it without causing a stir. It must have been extremely hush-hush even to the people around him.

"You'll see he was traveling a lot. Every time he went down to Phoenix, he took with him a contract to be signed, and every time he returned, he brought back a commission check. I have this gut feeling this Pinzer guy was somehow involved in the attacks on the businesses in your strip. I can't imagine Harold would allow violence. But I guess I really didn't know him very well, did I?" She took a long, thoughtful swallow from her glass and dabbed at her upper lip daintily to catch a drip of scotch left there. Helen stopped talking now. We were letting her words sink in. I looked at Van and then back down at all the documents.

Four hours later, around two o'clock in the morning, we had a plan. We'd go to the authorities and explain what Helen had found. We'd tell them together, stand together, because Helen had a huge stake in this, and Vanessa and I weren't going to let her go down alone for this if our suspicions were right. We figured Harold was somehow behind the whole thing. After going back and forth on the particulars several times, we finally agreed to meet at Helen's house the following morning at nine and drive down together.

****

I'd spent the morning with Gangster going over my lines, my part in the discussion. I kept repeating the facts as I knew them to be from my perspective—what Helen had told us sure seemed a viable reason for the brief crime spree felt by our little community.

But when I got to Helen's the next morning like we'd planned, she wasn't there. The door was locked, and the house was dark. I rang the doorbell, checked the backyard. Nothing. The garage was closed and when I looked into a window to see if her car was there, it was empty. No car either. I began to panic but then remembered Vanessa would be here shortly, too, and I needed to hold off making any assumptions about

Helen's whereabouts.

After thirty minutes, I started to worry again, so I left a note for Vanessa on Helen's front door:

I went home. Come meet me when you get this note. Where's Helen?

I got to my phone and immediately called Vanessa's house. Roberta answered the phone.

"Carlisle residence."

"Hi, honey. It's me. Is your mother there?"

"I thought she was meeting you and Helen?"

"Well, she didn't. I waited at Helen's a good thirty minutes. I'm a little frazzled, Roberta. Helen wasn't there either."

"Weren't you all supposed to meet at the police station? At least, I think that's where she said she was going? What's going on, anyway?"

"Oh, holy crap! I screwed up. I thought we were all supposed to meet at Helen's. Oh, thanks, Roberta. I spaced out one small little detail." My voice was strained but managed to have a sarcastic quality as well.

"Jeez, Georgie. I'm the one with amnesia but I remembered that!"

"Yeah, thanks. Gotta go. Talk to you later, honey. Bye." I'd successfully avoided telling Roberta what was happening, hopefully without offending her, and raced well over the speed limit to the police station. Helen and Vanessa were waiting for me outside.

****

"I never would've guessed, Helen." Vanessa was only learning the depth of Helen and only before her possible move away from here.

"She carries a journal around with her, Van."

"It's no big thing. I've only had one poem win

anything at all. But you're right; it's kind of exciting to see your work in print." Helen beamed through tired eyes.

We all drove over to the diner for a bite. It was Monday, a night we didn't have a dinner shift. So, we sat with the lights off in the bright sunlit room and made some sandwiches. We were all drinking iced tea; the caffeine boost was needed from the previous late night.

"Well, I think we did the right thing. The police will let us know their progress and hopefully we'll get to the bottom of this."

"I've been praying it turns out Harold isn't involved, but those documents look pretty damning."

"Well, make good on paying back those commissions and people will see what a decent person you are, Helen."

****

After we went our separate ways, I still felt my friends were close with me. I had a sense I'd always have them close one way or another, in my heart. When I got home and saw my message light blinking on the phone, I couldn't have been more pleased by the sound of the voice on the other end. But after I heard her words, I knew there was trouble brewing. The warm blush of camaraderie I'd felt just moments before was threatened in an instant by the nettling news she was leaving on my recorder.

Gangster flew from the bedroom into the kitchen to see me and rubbed against and through my legs.

"You hungry, buddy?" He purred out a yes. It'd been an entire day since I'd filled up his kibble bowl and only a few crumbs rested in its bottom. His water looked dingy and floated with hair and spittle from not refreshing it for over twenty-four hours, or was it the day before that? After tending to him, Gangster greedily ate the oily, fishy-smelling, crunchy nuggets, his head mantled over the bowl like he'd just killed another baby rabbit. When he was finished, he jumped back up onto the travertine countertop to offer his thanks. While I stroked his fur, one of my hands rested on the counter. It never ceased to amaze me how the marble stayed so cool in this desert's heat.

My other hand automatically joined the petting. His back arched along my fingernails as I scratched from his nose down his back and off the tip of his tail. He had a little knot of matted hair down near his rump, and my mind settled to a memory of how Bobby used to scratch my back for hours every Sunday morning without fail, our precursor to lovemaking. But then my mind wandered back to the blinking message. I'd had too many messages lately all delivering bad news. I wasn't sure I could handle any more trouble this soon.

Chapter 31

"We're here to speak with Mr. John Chariot. He's expecting us." Detective Mark had been with Sunnydale only a few years when his wife insisted, they move north out of the crime-laden city to a smaller town where the kids had a better chance of avoiding urban peer pressure. He and Willy met at Chariot with two Phoenix detectives he'd had the pleasure of working with during his stint here a few years back. They'd all first met at the station downtown to go over details of their impending interviews with Chariot and Pinzer.

"He'll be right with you." The receptionist remained cool even though she knew the men in front of her were officers of the law and even though Willy was donning his Sunnydale police uniform. She turned back to her keyboard and began typing without missing a beat. Another phone call and she pressed a button and spoke into her headset as she typed.

"Just a moment, please. May I say who's calling? Thank you." She pressed a code into the switchboard keys and transferred the call.

Just then, John Chariot came into the lobby and greeted the men. He shook each of their hands strongly and quickly.

"Hello, Detectives, Officer. Let's talk in the conference room, shall we? Tamara, hold my calls, please."

"Yes, Mr. Chariot."

Chariot turned and led the four men toward a lush room laden with leather and mahogany wood.

"Can I get you anything? Water, coffee?"

"Nothing, sir. We need to ask you a few questions. Will that be okay?"

"Absolutely. What can I help you with?"

"Are you familiar with the land purchase between Chariot and the town of Sunnydale?"

Chariot's face tightened and became red. He spoke, trying to mask his outrage with Pinzer. "Yes and no."

"Will you please explain what you mean, Mr. Chariot?" Detective Mark spoke deliberately and with little inflection.

"I remember one of my VPs was drawing up documents for its purchase. But I intercepted them because the property, the land, is corridor land. Our mission is to build boutique malls within areas with an already established demographic. We don't try to develop areas; we situate ourselves in already developed areas, like Phoenix, Carefree, Scottsdale, La Jolla, San Luis Obispo, areas like that. My mission has never been to try to develop a town, understand?"

"So, what you're saying is you didn't have knowledge of the purchase?"

"No, I did not. I told Zach to renege on the agreement. To tell the mayor we were going to have to pass. What has the mayor said about all of this? Did he say I was involved? Because if he did, he's lying. I never wanted this transaction to happen." Chariot was spilling like people do when the law is sitting staring them in the face.

"The mayor is dead."

"What?"

"He was killed in an automobile accident on his way to Sunnydale back from Phoenix."

"Oh, dear God."

Chariot seemed completely surprised by the mayor's death and sincerely angered about the land purchase. "So, sir, you knew nothing about this purchase. Money was exchanged, commissions paid."

"I only knew Zach wanted this. Nothing more. Do I need a lawyer?"

"If you feel you need one, sir. We're here to try and get to the bottom of a sudden burst of crime in Sunnydale. This information about the land just came to our attention yesterday."

"Well, talk to Pinzer. I had nothing to do with this."

****

Leyla leaned into Detective Mark seductively when she brought each of the men a bottle of water.

"Mr. Pinzer will be right with you, Officer." She said it close to his face.

"It's Detective." He spoke without humor and absent of facial expression. Leyla stood straight when he corrected her.

"Well, he'll be right with you, Detective." Her more professional demeanor returned upon Detective Mark's curt retort. The men all looked at each other when Leyla turned her back on them to head back to her desk.

Fifteen minutes passed and the men had yet to meet Zach Pinzer. He'd been hiding out in his office too long when the men waiting outside his door began to whisper quietly among themselves.

That's when Detective Mark stood and straightened his pants.

"Tell Pinzer we'll return with a warrant and compel him to meet with us, downtown." The others stood to leave when Leyla realized the seriousness of them being there.

"Wait just a minute, I'll call him again." She dialed his extension and turned away to whisper the urgent message. Then, she hung up the phone. "He said he'll be right out."

The men preferred to stand rather than sit again and looked impatient in the next few moments before Zach Pinzer appeared. He opened his door slowly, coolly. Pinzer appeared to Detective Mark clean-cut, perhaps too clean-cut.

"Gentlemen. So sorry about the delay. It's crazy here today. Do come in."

Detective Mark let the others enter Pinzer's office before following them. Zach held the door open and when they were all well inside, he followed them in.

"Leyla, hold my calls, will you?"

"Yes, Zach." She said it seductively and let their intimacy seep into the comment. Zach pressed a look at her meaning for her to stop. She looked at the papers in front of her when he closed the door behind him. Detective Mark caught it all and remained standing while Zach moved behind his desk, his barrier from the men in his office.

"I'm Detective Mark Dannon from Sunnydale. This is Officer Will Cleary from Sunnydale as well. These two gentlemen here are detectives from Phoenix PD, Detectives Steve Falk, and Tom Janzen."

"What can I do for you, gentlemen?"

"We have a couple of questions we hope you can shed a little light on."

"Shoot."

As Detective Mark began, he noticed a trashcan filled with shredded documents and a box next to it. Adjacent to the trashcan was the shredder idling and next to the shredder was another box with long shreds of paper spilling out onto the floor. He had a pair of scissors on his desk and whiteout next to the scissors. Pinzer's sleeves were rolled up just under his elbows and his hair looked damp around the edge of his reddened face.

"Been cleaning up?" Detective Mark pointed with his head to the shredding effort.

"Oh, that. Just some old papers I didn't need anymore. Old stuff."

"Is that why you kept us waiting outside? You were spring cleaning?" The questioning started out quickly and on a bad note.

"No, no. I was on a long-distance call."

"With whom?"

"Um, um. A guy in Nevada."

"What's this guy's name?"

"What can I help you with, gentlemen? It certainly mustn't be to learn about my latest sales call, is it?"

Detective Mark felt a pang in his gut, a pang he'd felt many times while standing face-to-face with a criminal. But this guy was more evil than the usual thug. He masqueraded daily as a businessman, the worst kind of criminal there was.

"Do you know Mayor Harold Pyle?"

"Hmm. A mayor, you say?"

"Yes. Mayor Harold Pyle. Know him?"

"Well, I believe I've heard of him. But I can't say I've ever made his acquaintance, no. Why?"

"Are you sure? We have a photo." Detective Tom Janzen pulled out a photo from the coroner's office and held it up to Pinzer.

"Oh, my goodness. He looks dead."

"That's 'cause he is."

"Oh my God."

"Recognize him?"

"Uh, no, no…I don't know." He sat slowly in his chair and looked as though he could vomit.

"You're sure you haven't met him?" Detective Mark pressed him harder.

"I told you no." Pinzer got visibly unsettled.

"Now, you see, that's funny. 'Cause we think you do know him, Zach." For the first time, Detective Mark got uncomfortably familiar with Pinzer.

"I'm calling my lawyer." He sat down and pulled himself tight against the desk. The interview stopped. They'd gotten enough information to dig deeper into the connection between Pinzer and Harold Pyle. Pinzer had lied and the police officers knew it. They still retained original copies of contracts signed by both men, copies of Harold's. They would connect Pinzer to the mayor and the mayor's meeting with him just before his untimely death. The other vehicle in Harold's automobile accident fled the scene. The accident was now under review. They believed it to be an intentional act of violence, and they were going to connect Pinzer to Harold's death. That's when Detective Mark spoke.

"See, Zach, it's like this. We know you were the last person to see the mayor alive. We also are looking into the car accident a little deeper. We don't think it was an accident at all." Zach's face was an open book of concern. He held his head up with his hand. "You see, we have eyewitnesses who saw the vehicle; we even have a partial plate. We're just steps behind the other person involved and we're closing in on him, Zach, fast." Mark continued after a meaningful pause. "So, you just call your lawyer. We'll all see how he handles the information."

Detective Mark gathered his team together and opened the door to leave. He let them shuffle out in front of him and moved to go, too, when he stopped, and stopped Willy with him. "Hold on, Will."

"Are mornings good for you, Zach? Or is it better to meet with you in the afternoon?" Then Detective Mark whispered something in Willy's ear and Willy went over to the wastebasket and boxes filled with destroyed paper.

"We'll be confiscating this as possible evidence." Willy doled out two of the three awkward containers to Falk and Janzen and they headed back out through the door past Detective Mark.

"It's garbage, right? Just think of it as us helping you clean your office!" Detective Mark winked, smiled at Pinzer, then shut the door behind him.

Chapter 32

"I'm here today to explain my involvement with the recent acts of my husband, the late Harold Pyle." Helen spoke nervously into the echoing microphone outside at the town's community center. She held a shaking piece of paper in her gloved hand as she talked. "I'm not here to make excuses for Harold. I only want you to know how deeply disturbed I am about the recent findings of his involvement with Mr. Zach Pinzer and Mr. Terrence "Tweeter" Wilson. It remains the detectives' findings, one, Mr. Zach Pinzer was the mastermind behind the entire plan to purchase property and businesses in our fine town of Sunnydale. Charges have been brought against both men in the crime to defraud the good people of Sunnydale as well as for the murder of my husband, Harold Pyle.

"I'll never understand what led Harold to become involved with such an underhanded plot. My only guess is money was at the heart of his crime. He received over one hundred fifty thousand dollars in what he called *commissions*. I have a check here in my hand to repay these commissions plus interest to the good people of Sunnydale. The money will be kept in trust fund and will be held for the future of preserving the land around our fine town.

"Again, I'm very sorry my husband had any involvement in this deceit. After Mr. Chariot and

Detective Mark say a few words, I will answer any questions you have." She stepped back from the podium and sat back down into her folding chair on the makeshift stage. John Chariot stood slowly and walked up to the microphone. He coughed before speaking.

"Hello everyone. Friends of Sunnydale, my company, Chariot International Incorporated, has become involved with a most heinous crime, the fraudulent transaction and transfer of land as well as a murder. Zachary Pinzer was the mastermind of this entire scheme of which I'm responsible only to the extent of allowing my vice president certain freedoms. We've already begun to establish more stringent internal controls over the authority of people in positions to act without my say-so. The money we received back from Sunnydale for the purchase of this land we're all standing on was over three million dollars. God bless you and your town for returning the fraudulent payments back to my company." Then he stood back a moment and coughed again into his fist. The crowd murmured during his pause. A light warm breeze kicked at the skirt of the podium and puffed through the microphone and out the speakers. Then, he straightened his back and spoke.

"However, in light of the loss your town has suffered directly because of my company. I am handing over the check to Mrs. Pyle to put in her preservation trust as a donation."

Helen's hands clasped together in amazement and her head dropped to her chest. The crowd gasped and a trickling clap began and filtered through the people until it built into a full-on burst of applause.

"Furthermore…Thank you, but it's truly not

necessary." He spoke over the crowd, "Thank you, please, thank you."

A sporadic clap lilted off until the last was heard.

Chariot continued, "When a business donates money or property there attaches with said donation a certain tax benefit, so, at the end of this year after my accountants calculate that benefit, my company will be writing another check for the trust. I'm thinking—"

The crowd burst quickly into another set of thunderous clapping. When it died down, he continued, "I'm thinking the check will be a six-digit figure, but again, the accountants need to be consulted about that." He chuckled and won over the star-struck audience with his charm and generosity. Then he stepped back, faced Helen and handed her the check. He sat down in the chair next to hers and held her with one arm around her shoulder in a show of unity. Helen continued to clap.

After that, Detective Mark got up to explain the details as much as he was free to. Then Helen fielded difficult questions from the audience, but she handled it like a queen. She was regal and honest, no less than any woman would be in a position of authority in the limelight. As she promised, she didn't make excuses. After all was said and done, she appeared innocent to the entire devious plot. Detective Mark cleared her name. She was free to leave with a few bruises. After she answered many questions, Helen did the most amazing thing.

"There's one more issue I'd like to take up with everyone gathered here today. Roberta? Are you here? Oh, there you are." Roberta looked at her mother and Vanessa shrugged her shoulders.

"You know, all of you, Ms. Roberta Carlisle-

Banner is a civil engineer, don't you? Now you see, that's exactly the degree a person managing a town or city should obtain. She's been very active her entire adult life in community service and a very active civil servant in her own right. One day after Harold died and not long after she'd been shot," Helen held her hand to her chest when she said those words and looked directly into Roberta's face, "we spoke about all sorts of things. One of those things Roberta revealed to me was a desire to do more for the community. *Become more active at the ground level* were her exact words. Do you remember, Roberta?"

She nodded her head, yes, she did remember.

"Well, I'm here with you all right now to propose we all stand behind Roberta Carlisle-Banner to nominate her officially as the new mayor of the town of Sunnydale." The crowd stood on its feet when she put out the motion. Roberta lost her composure, began to weep but very slightly, and held a hand to her mouth. "What do you say, Roberta? Will you consider it?"

Roberta beamed her joy at Helen and slowly nodded yes.

"There you have it, folks, our new mayor of Sunnydale!" The crowd roared and the small high school band began playing a lousy rendition of "Hooray for the Red, White, and Blue." Vanessa grabbed her daughter's arm and yanked it high over her head.

I was standing behind them in the audience. Roberta and Vanessa were holding hands and slowly moving between other audience members toward the stage, leaving me where I stood, for Roberta to make some unprepared speech about how she would work her hardest for the people. When she got up to the podium, she looked so very happy. In all my days here, she'd never beamed the way she did back then.

"Well! What a surprise." She put both her hands to her heart. Just then, Vanessa leaned into Roberta and whispered something in her ear. Roberta looked a little surprised but shook her head to indicate she agreed.

"Thank you all for such a wonderful moment." The clapping died down and she spoke sincerely. "First, I'd like to say how I wish someone else could be up here with me today. It's times like this, when something wonderful happens to you, you want to surround yourself with loved ones, the people who accept you no matter what."

Then, she paused, and I could hear the crowd whispering his name. *Bobby*.

She started up again after a fairly decent moment of anticipation. "So, I'm going to ask someone to join me and my mother. Someone who has been so very important in my life, for better and for worse, who is like a sister to me, and to whom I owe my life."

She was staring into my wet eyes, and I could see tears well up in hers all the way up there. "Georgie, will you come be with me too?" I couldn't handle it. I just busted out crying like a little girl, but I ran up to be with her—my friend, my sister. She hugged me and whispered *Thank you* in my ear. Vanessa and I stood together behind her with Helen at my other side. Roberta leaned into the microphone once more and said, "Thank you. If I'm elected…"

The crowd answered back, "When!"

"When I'm elected," she returned the positive statement, "I'll make you proud. Thank you all so very much." She stepped back and bowed. Then Helen grabbed her hand and held it high over her head. Roberta waved and blew kisses at everyone.

It was a glorious day.

Chapter 33

Well, as you might guess, Roberta was elected
Mayor of Sunnydale in the fall. We celebrated with red,
white, and blue streamers, hats, and those silly
noisemakers that roll out when you blow them into
colorful paper. Mr. Hanker's high school marching
band played up and down the streets of Sunnydale, and
we drank champagne and danced in the street. The
mood was hopeful and joyous. Everywhere Roberta
went, she locked my arm in hers to join her. We'd
scoop up Vanessa and the three of us paraded around
like Wynkin, Blynkin, and Nod. The only thing missing
was a rub-a-dub tub to float around in…and the water
in which to float, of course.

Vanessa turned to me at one point. She said, "I
wish Helen were here to see this."

Helen left late that summer—a good time to leave
the hot Arizona desert. She called a few times after
she'd reached Seattle. She found a houseboat on Lake
Washington and was enjoying the cool sea air blow
through her. She even went as far as to get a pet, a boat
cat. She called her Seabreeze.

Helen was writing the way she'd always hoped and
was becoming active with the local theatre, too, writing
plays and fiction. Her calls dwindled to once every
couple of weeks, then once a month; finally, they
stopped altogether shortly after Roberta's election in

Susan Wingate

November. Helen did call to congratulate her on her new career.

Roberta's first act as mayor was to set aside the land surrounding Sunnydale in order to purchase it with the money from the trust fund set up by Helen. She called the purchase the *Helen Pyle Preservation Land Trust* in honor of Helen.

****

After the election came the blur of Thanksgiving and Christmas, and we were looking toward a bright new year. Zach Pinzer and Tweeter were indicted in the murder of José and Harold and were sent away to serve life sentences.

The diner had a renewed surge of old-time customers from when Bobby and Vanessa were married. Vanessa would introduce me to them as one of her very best friends. Sunnydale finally started to feel like home. Until, of course, Vanessa told me about her cancer. Then Sunnydale started to feel like family.

Vanessa had gone back to Flagstaff, this time accompanied by me. As they rolled her along in a wheelchair, they had her in one of those insulting pieces of cloth they hand to patients and call robes. She looked pale. It was then I realized how sick she was.

"I haven't told Roberta yet, Georgie. I don't want to ruin it for her."

"You can't hide this from your own daughter, Van. You have to tell her."

"Well, when I decide to, will you be there with me? I don't think I can handle telling her alone, Georgie. I'd crumble."

"I'd be honored." She grabbed my hand in hers and kissed my knuckles.

"Hey! I have to pee." I ran out because I didn't want her to see me cry. She needed strong people around her through all this, not some sniveling, weepy thing. When I came back into her room the nurses were there marking up her breasts with a black marker. The radiation treatment only lasted a few minutes, but the laser and its effect subsequently burnt her skin raw.

When we got back to Sunnydale, I helped her get comfortable and sat with her for a bit before heading home. She told me to come by her house tomorrow at lunchtime and she'd have Roberta meet us there so she could tell her. I agreed.

Roberta was beside herself with worry. But the three of us held tight and promised no matter what, we'd stick together and make sure this thing, this cancer, didn't win out. She'd beat it once, and she could beat it again.

People tend to say things like that, you know, when they're faced with danger, more importantly when they're faced with fear and when around others. When we're alone, the panic and worry overcome us. It's only after we face the awful truth together, after the hours of consolation, do we really experience the terror laid before us. Later in the evening, after going our separate ways, I had a deep sense we were all crying in unison about some same fear we'd only moments before stood strong against collectively.

****

Vanessa made it through another year and the holiday season. By then, it was Thanksgiving Day. For this holiday, we all celebrated at Roberta's house. It was around three in the afternoon. I wore a cool, flowing dress so I could fill up on all Roberta's fine cooking. Vanessa looked like a hippy in a muumuu with her head wrapped elegantly in a scarf to hide her patchy hair.

Rick unexpectedly showed up at her doorstep with roses and chocolates. Roberta told him to go away after she took the flowers and candy and shut the door in his dumbfounded face. That's how she described the scene anyway.

"What are you doing here?" It wasn't the kindest welcome I'd ever heard.

Vanessa and I could hear them both from inside the house.

"You can't keep me away, Roberta. I love you! If you don't see me, I'm coming back tomorrow."

Vanessa and I were chuckling while we eavesdropped at the dining room table.

"I brought you a Thanksgiving gift," he said. "I know how much you love Thanksgiving, Rob." His voice sounded sweet and familiar.

Their divorce had been finalized the year before.

"Well, my family and I are having dinner. It wasn't right for you to just drop in." She was killing us. Van and I were sniggering like teenagers in the background.

"I'm sorry to interrupt, but I've been thinking about things, about us, you."

"Rick, really, I don't have time today. I have guests. Come back some other time." She'd opened the door, literally and figuratively, for another visit from him.

Roberta was in shock by his surprise appearance but recovered quickly after trying out one of the truffles.

She arranged the roses on our Thanksgiving table.

"Well, that's just lovely, isn't it?" She looked at us and we couldn't help but bust out from the entire episode.

"Shut up!" Roberta's smile veiled her true emotions. She was giddy.

Then we all sat down, just the three of us, together, for the last time.

Vanessa didn't even make it to the end of the year. We all spent Christmas by her bedside at the hospital, watching instruments pulse and ding, monitoring heart rate and pressure. We watched Van go in and out of consciousness, watched her wince in pain, and saw her thin skin receive yet another injection, another catheter, another line of fluids, morphine, and blood.

She said she couldn't do it anymore; she said she was sorry, but she wanted to die. So, she refused treatment. Vanessa wanted Roberta and me to take her home where she could die happy. She wanted no more interruptions from nurses, orderlies, and doctors…strangers. She only wanted her family around. That's what she told the doctor. She built up enough strength and we moved her into a wheelchair, got her into the car, drove her home, and got her comfortable.

She apologized to me. To me! For her treatment after she and Bobby divorced, up till not so long ago. I told her, "Don't do this." I said to her.

You see, from my point of view, I should've been apologizing to her. But then she said something I couldn't refuse. Vanessa had asked to talk with me alone, and excused Roberta from the bedroom.

"Georgie, if you hadn't come into town those many, many years ago and…stolen my husband away from me—" She tried to imitate Groucho, although it was a weak imitation, and she chuckled as she joked.

187

"—none of this would've happened." She made a low but sweeping gesture with her arm and continued to speak even though she was growing short of breath. "You and me, then you and Roberta. You saved her life, Georgie; I'm not sure it would've played out the same way if it were any different, you see? I'll never forget it. You saved the most important person in my life. And I love you for it. You need to understand this more than anything. Yes, I had my anger issues about Bobby but all of it peeled away in a flash the night Roberta got shot. You saved my baby, Georgie. Don't you ever forget how important you are to me, okay? Don't you ever doubt how much I love you, the here and now of it, okay?"

Her whispering voice sounded ministerial and profound. Words were lost for me.

"I want you to know something I've been keeping from you. You'll be angry. You will be. But after I tell you I hope you do the right thing by everyone concerned."

Vanessa piqued my curiosity. I couldn't imagine what she was going to tell me at this point. I wiped my nose with my hanky and looked at her, wondering what she would say next.

"Look, Bob was a loner more than you'll ever know now. He needed moments to himself." She paused to take a few deep breaths and then whispered the rest. "We don't have much time. Helen and Bob were close. Closer than you'll understand. They were like soul mates. I never understood either, until later." She breathed in and collected her strength. "Open the drawer there and hand me the letter with the initials H.M.W. on it."

I must have been sitting there blankly when she said, "Do it, Georgie, I don't have this kind of time." The letter was right on top of a stack of notepads. "Open it." She grabbed my hand when I started to. "Not now…after. Now you go get my girl. I need to talk to her."

"No, Van, not yet. Please." My sorrow felt like a mountain in my chest. I put my head on her hand, the one I'd been holding onto.

"Come on now, go. I need to talk to her. Now." My head shook yes but my body lingered then weakly moved. I stood and walked out to send in Roberta.

Seven minutes passed from the time I left to the time Roberta emerged.

My body was tucked, my head buried in my knees.

The letter was by my chair on the floor. When I looked up, I realized she'd left the door open. Her movement was lethargic, unsure. Her face had turned white.

Roberta said nothing. I didn't have to ask. She leaned against the wall of Vanessa's bedroom and covered her face.

Chapter 34

You know how you replay something in your mind you don't want to forget? That's what I do. But I parcel it out in slivers. I'm sure I've left out so much of this story. Some of the painful memories come when I least expect them and when they do, it seems I've been given some cosmic permission to talk about it, think about it, allowing me in steps to recall at first the most tranquil memories. Someday all the memories will reveal themselves. When that day comes, will it allow me to forget? Oh, I certainly hope not. But the mind is funny.

My mind settles every now and again on Helen, on the letter. In it, the writer refers to a past profession of love.

Dear Helen,

The time we've spent together is precious to me. I appreciate your words; you write like an angel. Please don't hate me, but I had to burn your note to me. When you expressed your feelings the other night, I reacted the way any man would who was approached by such a remarkable woman as you, Helen.

But we cannot continue.

I dearly love my wife. She's the most important thing in the world to me. Even though we didn't take things as far as we could have, I wanted to. But not for the reasons you might hope, for purely physical reasons, Helen. And you know as well as me, that's not fair to you, and it's most definitely not fair to Georgie.

To hear you express your love, well, your words fell over me like diamonds falling from a golden sky. Thank you. Thank you for feeling the way you feel about me. But I can't return the favor. I don't know what else to say.

Your true friend, Bob.

Was I angry? Hell, yes, I was angry. I felt duped. I felt like Helen was a fake. All those times we'd spent together—sharing, talking, laughing—they all meant nothing anymore. So, I wrote my own letter. All the anger I felt, from the start to the end, was expressed in my own letter. How when I first arrived no one could find the courtesy in their hearts to forgive me for taking Bobby away from Vanessa, how they refused to even talk to me, how they shunned me.

Well, Bobby left her. I never asked him to leave. Never.

I never expected him to come by the motel that night. He just appeared and I welcomed him in. I'll never be sorry. Vanessa didn't know, and Roberta won't ever hear it from my lips. One thing I learned from my momma was this: I never wanted to be like her and all those men. So, when Bobby came over, we talked for a good long time. I told him what he was doing was wrong. I told him he should go back to his wife and try harder. I told him he had a family who depended on him.

But he wouldn't hear it. He said the moment he saw me; he knew. He said he knew we would be in love. He didn't really have to talk anymore because the second I let him in my room I'd fallen in love with the man. I'd never felt anything so comfortable. I felt safe with him like toeing into a deep bathtub full of bubbles and sinking under for its protection. He was so handsome! And he had this rumbling deep voice, a voice that reverberated in my chest. He was right. How he could tell, I'll never know, but I fell in love with him right then, right there.

He had to talk me into the whole idea. I wasn't about to crumble like shortcake. He had to promise me I wasn't some fly-by-night sexual encounter and then goodbye. No sir. I even threatened him, told him if we were going to proceed with our relationship, it wasn't going to be some sleazy affair on the side. I told him if we were to make love, to consider it a contract. I told him I'd scream to the mountaintops if he woke up the next morning and figured he had made a mistake. He stayed with me until four in the morning. We only talked. When he went back to Vanessa's he told her he was leaving. Later in the morning, he brought his belongings and moved into the motel room with me.

After reading the letter Bobby wrote to Helen, I felt unwilling to forgive her. My response, from my enlightened viewpoint, was to be mailed to her the following day. Shock is a funny thing. It wears off. When it does, it leaves you open to many ideas. It's like waking and pulling off the covers in the morning. So after sleeping on it, I wrote another one, in it I described my surprise and hurt, but also my forgiveness.

People have so many stories in them, some so beautiful and filled with longing and hope you want to hear it repeated over and over. Many of the stories no one would ever want to hear, let alone tell. It makes me wonder about Helen's stories.

I also wonder what the story is like for Roberta—what she tells Rick. She called the other morning and told me they were considering the possibility of adoption. They want a baby. Maybe it wasn't necessary, but I gave her my blessing. I think Vanessa allowed me the right. She probably giggled from above at my courage. Anyway, I've kind of grown on Roberta—like moss!

So here I am now in one of the most desolate parts of the country. Dry, dry Arizona. Here, I've found myself a well, an oasis, a lifeline—my only true family where I buried my husband, and then my sister.

You know, one day I was pulling weeds in the garden and flipping them outside the fence. The gate was open. I didn't hear or see anything around me; I was in a weed-pulling zone. Anyway, this young deer had wandered down from the hills, probably a good mile off her migration path. That's what they normally did; stay away like that. But this one was different. She made her way in through the open gate.

My thoughts were elsewhere. I wasn't paying any attention to anything when I felt this breath close to my back as I yanked out a dandelion. It wasn't so long since Bobby had died so I said, "Bobby?" I still missed him very much and the garden always made me think of him. We loved our garden and it still showed. Maybe the doe's instinct sensed it was shelter.

Anyway, she came up on me while I was kneeling. When I felt her breath, I straightened my back when I realized that, of course, it wasn't Bobby behind me. It wasn't anything human. I turned very, very slowly. She was so scrawny. She didn't have antlers, so I assumed it was a female. After further inspection, if you know what I mean, I saw I was correct in my assumption. She puffed out a little blast of air again and walked cautiously around toward my hand holding the dandelion. I didn't move, didn't utter a sound. In fact, I think I was holding my breath.

She lifted her head, maybe in our recognition of each other, and then she almost pointed to the dandelion with her wet snout. She looked awfully thin and so delicate. She looked hungry.

"Do you want this?" The words I uttered were barely audible, even for me to hear. When I asked her, she didn't answer, of course, but instead she put her head low like she understood, you know? I raised my hand slowly so I wouldn't startle her. She approached tentatively, carefully, keeping her entire body, everything but her head, a safe distance from me. Her snout felt warm and wet against my palm as she nibbled right from my hand. I felt like God was blessing me for something. I didn't know what. He'd forgiven me for all of my sins right then and there. That's how it felt. Amazing. It was something else.

After the doe took her morsel of food, she did the sweetest, most delicate thing—she nuzzled and licked my hand. "You're welcome." Our eyes connected and the world spun away from me. I'd never had anything so pure happen. I was stunned but went back to pulling my weeds. She continued through the garden with me. But she was making no visible decisions to eat just the weeds. She ate everything. Anything she wanted. And you know what? I let her.

Looking back, I think the doe came to me because someone—God, I suppose, or whatever your version of God is—wanted me to understand I wasn't alone anymore in Sunnydale. I had Bobby, yes, and Vanessa and Roberta, even Helen. We had experienced some hard times, bumpy times, with each other. There'll be more, you can bet on it. But we overcame our obstacles. We hurt. We cried. We yelled at each other. We cried more. We tried to hurt one another with actions and words. We realized so many things about each other but in the end, we had no visible scars, no bruises, and no long-lasting pain. We're all scrawny does, hungry for something.

Our time together became mundane, every day, pedestrian even. How can I say this...well, our normalcy became fundamental to our relationship. We became family.

Then another miraculous thing happened. It was slow, subtle, and took its time, but we missed each other when we were apart. I needed Vanessa so much and she needed me. I missed Roberta, too, but with her it was different, more like a cousin. Not now, of course. Now we're closer than that, but for a time Roberta and I were like cousins. However, Vanessa and I shared so much—Bobby, divorce, death, pain, loss, memories, the diner, cooking, business, shopping—so much. Our relationship settled into something beautiful, easy, soft to the touch, you know? Like that kiss from the doe— sweet, gentle, and perfect. Vanessa became my family, and I became hers.

We talked endlessly about the course of our lives, how things happened, what we would do differently. But we knew if we changed one iota on the road to where we were, we wouldn't be the same. Neither one of us wanted that. We wanted each other just the way we were—full of faults, errors, bad judgment,

Susan Wingate

kindnesses, honesty, growth, compassion, and willingness to explore. We knew we had value, if only to each other, we had value.

Vanessa made me promise when she died I would spend more time with Roberta. I gladly gave her my promise. See, God has this little secret. He knows even when you're alone if you have family you're always loved. I think that should be the first commandment in the Bible, but I didn't write His book. Can you imagine? I think there would be only one rule if I wrote the Bible. It would go like this: *Love every living thing.*

All people, not only blood relations, can be family. It's our choice to include or exclude people, to love or to hate. It's a conscious choice, a conscious decision. After all these years, I believe a person has infinite space to tuck yet another somebody into their heart. A person can love many, many people all at once. Aren't we lucky for that? Think about the exponential effect if we only took ten someones into our hearts. A net would be cast out from us, and from those ten, ten others would be cast, and again and again, until the web would be huge and buoy us, lifting humanity hundreds and hundreds of rungs higher on the ladder of compassion. Now, wouldn't that be wonderful.

Tonight, as I remember Vanessa's funeral, my eyes are fading. Tomorrow and for a week to come, we won't open the diner, out of respect. We've had a death in the family. We're going to revel in our thoughts of life with her and without her. We're going to suffer and celebrate, cry, and laugh, hope and fear, and we'll be more human for it. After all, I can't help believing in humanity. People will be born, fall in love, and die. Rinse and repeat, all of it over and again. You see, the future will be bright because we've built our family. We've built a catch net.

A word about the author...

Susan Wingate writes unputdownable, surprising and twisty stories, with crackling dialogue, that exhibit a rare deftness in style, offering up stories that are riveting, original, and with a humanity rarely seen in contemporary fiction.

Winner of Best Fiction for *How the Deer Moon Hungers* in the 2020 Pacific Book Award, Susan Wingate is a #1 Amazon bestselling author of over fifteen novels.

Visit her at:

http://www.susanwingate.com

www.ingramcontent.com/pod-product-compliance
Lightning Source LLC
Chambersburg PA
CBHW070123260626
47160CB00004B/1597